ANDERTON JUSTICE

Cowboy Tom Hall awakes after a drinking spree to discover he has been appointed marshal of Anderton, a frontier town split by rivalry between townsfolk and homesteaders. The new judge, an attractive young woman, arrives in town, and on the same stage is the mysterious gunslinger Mort Lazarus. A massacre of townsmen by homesteaders leaves Anderton at the mercy of Lazarus and his outlaw friends, and only an unlikely alliance can prevent further bloodshed. Even so, the odds are stacked against Hall.

Books by Robert Eynon
in the Linford Western Library:

JOHNNY ONE ARM
GUNFIGHT AT SIMEON'S RIDGE
BROTHERS TILL DEATH
PECOS VENGEANCE

ROBERT EYNON

ANDERTON JUSTICE

Complete and Unabridged

LINFORD
Leicester

First published in Great Britain in 1997 by
Robert Hale Limited
London

First Linford Edition
published 2001
by arrangement with
Robert Hale Limited
London

British Library CIP Data

Eynon, Robert
    Anderton Justice.—Large print ed.—
    Linford western library
    1. Western stories
    2. Large type books
    I. Title
    823.9'14 [F]

    ISBN 0–7089–4578–3

Published by
F. A. Thorpe (Publishing)
Anstey, Leicestershire

Set by Words & Graphics Ltd.
Anstey, Leicestershire
Printed and bound in Great Britain by
T. J. International Ltd., Padstow, Cornwall

Dedicated to
My friends at Treorchy Carpets

1

The town barber was holding forth to a small group of customers about how he would put a rapid end to the troublesome Indian wars in North Dakota, when the door of the shop opened to reveal a well-built but trail-dusty cowboy in his late twenties.

The barber moved his cutthroat razor away from the lathered face of the client seated in the swivel chair, and turned to greet the newcomer.

'You need a shave and a trim, young feller,' he commented cheerfully. 'There's the price list on the wall, right next door to the mirror.'

The cowboy scratched his stubbly chin thoughtfully, but shook his head.

'I got something to pawn,' he said with a hint of embarrassment in his voice. 'It's a gold watch — solid gold. I heard you deal in that kind of thing.'

He had the watch ready in his hand, and offered it to the barber, who tossed the razor to one side and carefully wiped his hands on his apron.

'OK, let's see what you got there, son,' he said. 'Is it working?'

'Sure, like a clock,' the cowboy replied without thinking.

The customers laughed, and a foam bubble formed on the lips of the man in the chair. The cowboy blushed; he obviously wasn't used to pawning his possessions.

The watch felt heavy in the barber's hand. He raised it to his ear and listened to the ticking.

'I'll give you four dollars for it,' he announced.

The cowboy's face fell. He'd been hoping for more than four dollars.

'Could you raise that a few dollars, mister?' he mumbled? 'You can see it's a good watch.'

'Sure it's a good watch,' the barber agreed. 'I could fill a barn with the good watches I been offered in this

town. Now, do you want the four dollars?'

The cowboy nodded his head without enthusiasm. The barber pocketed the time-piece and scooped some coins from his day's takings.

'Anything else you want to pawn, cowboy?' he enquired. 'Your horse, maybe?'

The stranger gave him a pained look.

'My horse went lame outside Pueblo,' he said. 'I already sold the saddle.'

The barber nodded sympathetically. He almost regretted having quibbled over a couple of dollars.

'Why don't you take a look in at the Golden Fleece dance hall,' he suggested. 'Miss Millie can sometimes find a few hours' work for fellers who are just drifting through.'

The cowboy mumbled his thanks for the advice and made for the door. Outside the sun was setting and the shops were starting to close. At the last moment the barber called him back. There was an honesty in the cowboy's

3

face that made him feel sorry for the young feller's plight.

'If you're lucky,' the barber told him, 'ask Miss Millie for an advance so that you can redeem the watch. If you get the money to me by sunset tomorrow, I'll only charge you a quarter!'

* * *

Anderton seemed to be a growing township with plenty of shops that attested to its prosperity. It was named after a trail boss who'd been crushed under the wheels of a wagon driven by his own son. The son still lived in the town, a small, wizened old man who could recount the incident as if it had happened yesterday or at most a week ago.

The town boasted two saloons: the Golden Fleece the barber had spoken about, and a larger, newer, more sumptuous building called the Rockingstone Hotel. As he walked along the main street the cowboy spotted an old

adobe jailhouse on the corner of one of the blocks. Next to it a wooden shopfront was in the process of being painted with the words, *Judge Deneuve, Attorney*.

The cowboy was more interested in the jail-house and its incumbent. He fingered the coins in his pocket and wondered what the town marshal was like. The personality of the marshal could make a lot of difference to someone like himself who was just passing through and lacked the money to hire a room for the night.

A good marshal would overlook his soiled clothing and treat him with courtesy, whereas a bad lawman would view him with distaste and suspicion, and might go out of his way to give him a bad time.

The jailhouse told him nothing; its front door was slammed shut and its front window was grimy. It looked deserted. He passed it by, and made for the Golden Fleece at the far end of the street.

There were about a dozen customers in the saloon when he went in. They were sitting round in small groups, playing cards or just drinking and talking. At the counter stood a huge bartender who was completely bald. The cowboy walked over to him and ordered a glass of beer, that he knew would have to last him a long time.

'Is the owner here?' he enquired as the bartender drew the beer with a hand as big as a shovel.

The bald man thought about it for a moment, the effort apparent on his face.

'She's upstairs,' he replied slowly. 'With the girls. They'll be coming down to dance later on. You'll like the dancing. All the fellers do.'

'You hear that, boys?' a voice hollered. 'There's gonna be dancing girls tonight. Yippee!'

The cowboy half turned to where a group of men were sitting drinking whiskey from bottles, and already looked rather bleary-eyed. They wore

ragged dungarees and were obviously in town from the countryside for the night. At the mention of the dancing girls they became animated and none too guarded with their comments.

The huge bartender gave the cowboy a sad glance.

'They're homesteaders,' he said. 'Sometimes they give the girls a hard time. I hope I ain't gonna have to throw them out tonight. They ain't bad fellers on the whole, and they always come back to say they're sorry for what they done. It's just that Miss Millie don't like anyone pawing the girls.'

'It's Miss Millie I wanted to see,' the cowboy said. 'I'm told she sometimes takes help on. I need work.'

The bartender wiped a glass on a white cloth, taking care not to crush it between his stubby fingers.

'Miss Millie won't see you without,' he said. 'That's if you're an honest feller, of course.'

'Sure,' the cowboy agreed, regretting that he knew nobody in town who

could attest to his integrity.

The door of the salon swung open again and a middle-aged man strode in, wearing a grey frock-coat and silk waistcoat, and tapping the floorboards jauntily with a cane as he walked along.

'Is Miss Millie upstairs?' he enquired of the bartender, who drew to a respectful attention behind the counter.

'She sure is, Mr Tanner,' the big man replied. 'She's putting the finishing touches to the girls' dresses.'

The newcomer began to climb the stairs in sprightly fashion, and the bartender turned back to the cowboy.

'That's Mr Tanner,' he said. 'He runs the bank. He's a real gentleman. By the way, mister, you gotta name?'

'Sure,' the cowboy smiled. 'Name's Hall, Tom Hall.'

The big man glanced across at the group of homesteaders who were getting noisier every moment. Then a flurry of applause broke out from the rest of the drinkers. The girls were on their way down the stairs, lips crimson

and cheeks rouged. A woman in her forties, but still attractive, ushered them down the carpeted staircase to the raised stage at the end of the saloon.

'Bert!'

The sharpness of Miss Millie's voice jolted the pianist, who'd been half asleep over his whiskey bottle. He rose unsteadily from the table and lurched over to the piano, which he proceeded to play with surprising gusto.

The girls responded with a lively routine under the watchful gaze of the proprietress. The customers whooped and yelled their appreciation, but unfortunately the homesteaders, who were nearest the stage, were too drunk to appreciate the finer points of the display. One of them managed to lean forward and dispossess one of the dancers of a shoe, while another tried to clamber onto the stage holding a liquor bottle in his hand.

The atmosphere in the hall changed as the customers at the back ordered the homesteaders to quit their tomfoolery

and sit back down. Inevitably a skirmish started between the two factions, and the next moment the huge bartender was among the troublemakers, trying to minimize the damage to limbs and furniture. Miss Millie was close at his heels, shouting abuse at the homesteaders while the pianist continued a honky-tonk medley as if nothing was happening.

Tom Hall saw a chair swung in the air; it crashed down on the back of the big man's head and he hit the floor with a thud. Meanwhile, deprived of her protector, Miss Millie was being thrown about in the throng like a rag doll.

It would have been wiser for Hall to drink up and leave, but he shared the westerners' distaste for ill-manners towards the fair sex. Besides, he enjoyed a good fight now and again so he made his way to Miss Millie's side, flattening anyone who got in his way with fists hardened by prairie life.

A gunshot startled the combatants, who froze on the spot. Tom Hall looked up and saw Tanner standing at the top

of the staircase, with a smoking revolver in his hand. At the same moment the cowboy felt a hand tugging at his shirtsleeve. He turned round and found himself confronted by the bartender, who'd risen to his feet but looked shaky and confused.

Hall was about to ask him if he was all right, when the big man suddenly threw a straight right hand at his jaw. The punch only travelled a foot or so, but for Tom Hall every light seemed to go out — in the saloon, in the town, in the whole world.

2

He woke up once during the night, but his head ached so bad he couldn't raise it from the bunk where someone had laid him. He'd had a series of vivid dreams in which he'd been drinking and carousing to the familiar chords of the honky-tonk piano. He peered upwards and saw no stars; at least he was under cover, and not lying on damp earth. He closed his eyes and went back to sleep.

When he next opened his eyes it was daylight. He felt terrible. He moved his head gingerly to one side and focused on the iron bars separating him from the rest of the room. It dawned on him that he was in a cell. The town marshal was not such a nice feller after all.

There was nobody he could call out to. He struggled into a sitting position, feeling parched and very wretched.

Outside in the street the township of Anderton was coming to life, with the sound of children's voices as they made their way to school, and the clatter of horses and carts as the residents began their day's trading.

The jailhouse door opened and a familiar figure appeared. It was Tanner, the banker. He was dressed sombrely in a black suit, white shirt and grey tie as if on his way to a funeral or the public trial of a debtor.

'How are you feeling today, Hall?' he enquired bluffly. 'I should imagine your head must feel pretty bad.'

Tom Hall stroked his forehead and felt a throbbing pulse trying to get out.

'It does,' he admitted. 'I took one hell of a punch from that bartender.'

The bank manager laughed.

'You seemed to get over the punch pretty quickly,' he said. 'Though you did look dazed for a while. I reckon it was Millie's liquor that got you in the end.'

'You mean, I went on drinking after I came to?'

'Sure you did, but only till around midnight. I guess you'd had enough by then.'

'And that's when the marshal threw me in jail?' Hall asked.

'Nope,' Tanner corrected him. 'That's when Joel — he's Millie's bartender — carried you over here. Millie was happy for you to stay in her place, but no, you kept on about real cowboys hating feather mattresses, so in the end they brought you here just to shut you up.'

'So I ain't under arrest?'

The banker shook his head and pushed the cell door open to prove his point. 'Well, I must be going,' he announced. 'The bank's already open. By the way, your gun and badge of office are in the desk drawer.'

Tom Hall stared at him.

'Badge of office?' he said.

'Don't you remember?' Tanner smiled. 'Last night you agreed to act as temporary town marshal until we can hold a proper election the beginning

of next month . . . '

The new marshal was still sitting on the cell bunk when Joel, the giant bartender, arrived bearing fresh water in a bucket and a mug of hot coffee with a hunk of dry bread.

'From Miss Millie,' he said simply, and watched as Tom Hall splashed the water over his face and neck and then devoured the bread and coffee.

'The last town marshal,' Hall said after a while. 'What did he die of?'

'He didn't die,' Joel answered reassuringly. 'He just lost his nerve and rode off one day. Anderton can be a pretty lively place for one man to keep law and order.'

'What makes it so lively?' Tom Hall asked. 'I mean, who causes the trouble?'

'It's usually between the homesteaders and the townsfolk,' Joel said. 'The townsfolk say the homesteaders ain't civilized, and the homesteaders reckon the townsfolk are too smart for their own good. Then there's Mr Fisher . . . '

'Who's he?'

15

'He's got a big spread to the east of Anderton, but he's always looking for more land to buy up and he kinda takes it personal when the homesteaders refuse to sell up and move on.'

'So he's a rancher,' the marshal remarked.

'Kind of, but he lives right here in town with his wife and two kids. He leaves the ranching side of things to his foreman and men who know about that side of things.'

The big man fished in his pocket and produced a piece of notepaper.

'I nearly forgot,' he said. 'Mr Tanner gave me this for you. Said he wouldn't have time to tell you everything before the bank opened.'

Hall opened the piece of paper and read. The note contained two instructions: Meet Judge Deneuve off the stage at noon. Stand up to Will Fisher if he tries to push you around.

'What's this about a judge?' he asked Joel.

'There's a new judge arriving on the

stage-coach,' the big man said proudly. 'We ain't never had a judge of our own before. The townsfolk are pretty excited about it. They reckon the new feller will soon put an end to the squabbling in these parts.'

'Where's he from?' the marshal asked.

'Louisiana,' Joel said. 'Mr Fisher's got some contacts there and they put an advertisement in one of the newspapers. Judge Deneuve was the only one who wanted to come this far west. So far everything's been done by letter, so nobody knows if the new judge is an old feller or still wet behind the ears. We've all been betting on it.'

Marshal Tom Hall gave a yawn. 'I've got an idea Joel,' he said.

'What's that, Marshal?'

'You go and meet the judge off the stage. That way you'll be the first to know if you've won your bet or not!'

3

The new lawman was feeling almost human again by the time his next visitors arrived. There were two of them: a short, dapper man who looked as if he was used to giving orders, and a much younger man who resembled him, but was taller and bigger built. Unfortunately, the youngster's advantage in stature was diminished by the weakness of his chin and the shiftiness of his expression.

The older man glared at Tom Hall as if he was a toad that had just emerged from under a stone.

'So you're the new town marshal,' he observed scornfully. 'By God, Tanner sure knows how to pick them!'

Hall didn't need the banker's scribbled message to take a dislike to a man like this.

'I take it you're Mr Fisher,' he said

coldly. 'Mr Tanner told me to expect you sooner or later.'

'You'd better show my pa some respect,' the younger man warned him. 'You can get up off your backside for a start.'

The lawman remained unmoved and neither of the visitors pressed the point.

'Tanner's action in appointing you was quite undemocratic,' the elder Fisher pointed out.

Hall made as if to remove the tin star from his shirt. Fisher went on hurriedly, 'However, since the post is vacant I've no objection to you remaining in office until the town council holds a proper election,' he said.

'But you'd better keep your nose clean, mister,' Fisher Junior broke in again. 'This town ain't short of men who could wear that badge in your place.'

Tom Hall didn't even bother to reply. It was up to Will Fisher to slap the youngster down when he spoke out of turn. The kid was obviously spoilt rotten.

In the distance they could hear whooping and shouting.

'What time you got, Tess?' Fisher asked his son.

'Coming up noon, Pa.'

'That'll be the stage with the new judge on it,' Will Fisher informed the marshal. 'You should be there to meet it.'

'I already deputized Joel from the Golden Fleece to go meet the stage,' Hall said with a hint of a smile.

Will Fisher didn't like the man's nonchalance which bordered on insolence. 'Well, you tell the judge to report to me as soon as he's settled in,' he said. 'I'll be at home; everybody knows where that is.'

Without further ado father and son walked out of the little jailhouse, leaving the door gaping behind them. From the comfort of his chair, the marshal could survey the length of the street as far as the Rockingstone Hotel where the coach had halted. He could see the big man, Joel, hovering at the

door of the coach.

A lithe, rangy man was talking to Joel. Must be the new judge, Hall thought approvingly. Even from that distance the feller looked as if he could be useful. Meanwhile, the stage driver was bringing down baggage from a slip of a girl wrapped in a black travelling cloak.

For the next few minutes he busied himself counting the six-gun and shotgun cartridges in the various drawers of the desk. Then Joel came back, closing the door behind him.

'Judge didn't make it,' he announced. 'There was only one feller on the stage. I didn't like the look of him, Marshal. He looks like trouble.'

The lawman stared at him. 'What do you mean?' he asked.

'Dunno. It was just the way he looked at me. Made my flesh creep.'

Tom Hall shook his head. That was all he needed — a giant of a man who could flatten you with a blow yet be frightened by a man's gaze.

'Thanks anyhow, Joel,' he said. 'You can go now. I guess we can make do without a judge until the next stage rolls in.'

A few minutes after the big man's departure he was summoned by a knock at the jailhouse door. The two passengers off the stage were standing there. The tall, lithe man fixed the lawman with a fathomless gaze that seemed to read his mind. Uneasily, Tom Hall turned his attention to the beautiful young lady at his side. She was clearly very angry, and the anger added colour to her cheeks and to her loveliness.

'That oaf of a man you sent to meet me,' she blurted out. 'He didn't even ask me who I was. If it hadn't been for Mr Lazarus here, I'd have been left stranded in the street.'

The tall man flashed her a smile that still couldn't bring warmth to his expression.

'It was a pleasure, Miss Deneuve,' he said. 'And so was your company

throughout the journey. I shall be staying a week or two in Anderton, and hope to see you frequently if you are not too busy.'

He moved off with the menacing grace of a mountain cat. Meanwhile, Tom Hall was at a loss as to what to do next.

'Deneuve,' he said awkwardly. 'Are you belonging to the new judge we were expecting?'

'I am the new judge, Marshal,' she informed him. 'Now will you escort me to my hotel so that I can freshen up!'

4

Tom Hall was rather surprised to receive an invitation to supper at Tanner's house the following evening. He had just enough warning to handwash a shirt and brush down a pair of breeches to look presentable for the occasion.

It was an intimate gathering. Miss Millie was there and the foursome was completed by Miss Deneuve, who had taken up residence at the Rockingstone Hotel. Miss Deneuve looked stunning in a simple green dress that set off her flowing brown hair and olive-smooth complexion.

Anderton's new judge insisted on being addressed as Jo, which was short for Joanne. Miss Millie took advantage of the occasion to find out as much as she could about the young girl from Louisiana.

'My parents are of French descent,' Jo explained obligingly. 'When the Civil War broke out between the Union and the Confederacy, they decided to send me to stay with relatives near Paris, France. There I lived in a small château and had a private tutor. When the war ended I came back home. All the former staff of my father's legal firm had either been killed or wounded, so I began to help him in the business, though I was still only in my early teens. I learned quickly and rose to the position of junior partner. But then I saw Mr Fisher's advertisement in the newspaper . . . '

The banker gave a little cough.

'Actually, it was the town council's idea,' he corrected her. 'Fisher only *thinks* he runs Anderton.'

'What do you think of Will Fisher?' Millie asked with a twinkle in her eye. 'How did he react when he learned that the new judge was a woman?'

'I suspect that it came as a shock to him at first,' Jo said diplomatically, as

she recalled the unpleasant scene at Fisher's house. 'But the whole town seems intrigued by the novelty. People have been coming and staring through my office window all day. As for Mr Fisher, he's a man of strong ideas, and rather set in his ways. I had to point out to him that I am here to serve the community, not individual interests.'

Millie and Tanner nodded their heads approvingly. Jo Deneuve clearly had strong ideas of her own.

'By the way, Mr Tanner,' Jo asked suddenly. 'What is your background?'

Before the banker could answer, Millie had beaten him to it.

'Oh, Ian is quite a mystery,' she grinned. 'He'd already been here a few years when I arrived, but nobody could tell me much about him. He'd just turned up in town with a solid bankroll and opened the first credit house Anderton had ever possessed. He staffed it with strangers, too, old acquaintances from his travels, men

no longer young but sharp with figures and able to handle the public well.'

'And you, Miss Millie?' Tom Hall enquired, determined not to be left out of things.

'Me?' Millie laughed lightly. 'I'm just a dancer turned manager. I didn't want the younger girls to be exploited like I was so I formed a travelling troupe of my own. We've been here two years now, which is our record.'

'But you mean to move on again?' Jo Deneuve asked her.

This time it was the banker's turn to intervene.

'That's a sore point,' he said frankly. 'I've done my darndest to persuade Millie to settle down here, and that includes an offer of marriage that I've repeated on more than one occasion.'

Millie leaned across and squeezed Tanner's hand affectionately.

'Ian,' she said with a sad smile, 'you know that I can't settle down

when there's a whole world out there. I admire a man like the marshal there, who's a born drifter. I should have been a man. Life would have been easier for me.'

'But there's plenty going on in Anderton,' Tanner objected. 'Why, only next Saturday Will Fisher's holding a barbecue on his spread and we're all expected to be there.'

Jo Deneuve looked anxiously at the clock. 'I almost forgot,' she said. 'I promised to meet Mr Lazarus at the Rockingstone after supper. I'd better be on my way. Thank you for a lovely evening.'

The marshal rose to his feet at the same time. 'It's dark,' he told the girl. 'I'll walk you to the saloon.'

Before they left, Tanner called Tom Hall back for a quiet word. 'Lazarus,' he said. 'Is that the feller who got off the stage? I thought I knew him from somewhere.'

Hall waited for him to go on.

'Mort Lazarus is a variety of things,'

the banker went on. 'A confidence trickster, gigolo, thief, hired gun — and above all a killer. You're only going to be marshal for a few weeks, Tom. Try to keep out of his way!'

5

Tom Hall spent the next few days helping Jo Deneuve to settle into her new office on Anderton's main street. The proximity in which they worked, erecting shelves and moving desks around, made the shy marshal uncomfortably aware that the young lady judge was casting a spell upon him, though for her part Jo was much too preoccupied with her new post to pay any attention to her eager helper's feelings.

As a cattle drover Hall had mainly been acquainted with bar hall girls who always exacted a price for their briefly bestowed favours. Miss Deneuve was something quite different, and the lawman had to steel his nerve before asking her for the pleasure of her company at the barbecue at Will Fisher's ranch.

As it happened, somebody else had beaten him to the draw.

'I'm sorry, Tom,' Jo Deneuve told him cheerfully. 'Mr Lazarus asked me the same question last night over dinner, and I had no reason to refuse him.'

Hall fingered his stetson awkwardly in his hand. Mort Lazarus was also staying at the Rockingstone Hotel and had plenty of opportunity to foster his friendship with the girl from Louisiana.

'That's fine then,' he managed to smile. 'Maybe a dance then, if you've got the time. Not that I'm much of a dancer,' he added quickly.

That was true. From an early age he'd had to fend for himself on the range, where social graces had a very low priority.

She returned his smile, quite oblivious to the growing emotion inside him. 'I'm sure I'll have time,' she told him. 'Especially for you, Tom.'

★ ★ ★

The Fisher spread was less than five miles outside town. The ranch-house was situated in a pleasant, fertile valley watered by a healthy arroyo and populated with verdant deciduous woodland. As he rode up to the ranch the marshal wondered why Will Fisher chose to reside in Anderton rather than these idyllic surroundings. He could only surmise that Fisher was a man who wanted to keep his finger on the pulse of the growing township that offered so many possibilities for enrichment.

Fisher was standing near a table laden with food and drink. A lot of guests had arrived already and were milling about in the yard in front of the ranch-house. In one of the empty corrals a group of musicians were tuning up for the long night ahead.

The petite, pretty woman at Fisher's side introduced herself to the new lawman as the rancher's wife and the hostess for the evening. Also there was Tim Riley, the plump, garrulous Irish-man who owned the Rockingstone

Hotel. He and Tom Hall nodded to one another courteously as Mrs Fisher asked the marshal what he'd like to drink.

'I'll have a beer, if that's all right, ma'am,' he replied.

'And make it your last,' Will Fisher told him sharply. 'The homesteaders and their offspring have already started to show up. It wasn't my idea to invite them,' he said, glaring at his wife. 'If they behave themselves they can stay; if not, that's where you come in, Marshal.'

Hall nodded. It was no great sacrifice. He'd never been a heavy drinker and the thought of the night at the Golden Fleece still haunted him. He could only suppose that Joel's haymaker had robbed him of all his inhibitions.

A buggy came rolling in through the gate amidst a flurry of chicken and geese who'd strayed into its path. Everybody turned to look at the new judge and her companion. Strangely, it was Mort Lazarus who seemed to catch

the attention of the crowd. He was as taut as a coiled spring in a black suit that showed up his twin pearl-handed Colt .45s. His movements were precise yet easy as he helped Miss Deneuve to descend from the buggy.

'Fine feller, that Lazarus,' Fisher remarked to Tom Riley. 'A useful man to have around the place.'

'Sure is, Will,' the Irishman agreed with complete disregard for the presence of the town marshal. 'He's the kind of man who'd clean up a town in an afternoon.'

By the time Tanner and Miss Millie arrived, driven by Joel the bartender, the music and dancing were well under way.

The banker made his way to Tom Hall's side as Mort Lazarus and Jo Deneuve spun by, carried along by the tempo of the fiddles.

Tanner watched them with a jaundiced eye. 'It's strange,' he said out of the corner of his mouth. 'Our young lady judge could probably read and

fathom out any lawbook you put in front of her, yet she can't see through Mort Lazarus at all.'

Prominent among the younger dancers was a girl with striking blonde hair and long, shapely legs who seemed intent on collecting as many dancing partners as she could in the course of the evening. In fact, the only man she danced with on more than one occasion was Will Fisher's son, Tess.

'That's Jed Stacey's daughter, Greta,' Tanner said. 'She lives with her father on one of the homesteads.'

'She's enjoying herself,' Hall remarked, and realized suddenly that Mort Lazarus was spoiling the night for him.

'She always does,' Miss Millie retorted as she came over to hand Tanner a fresh drink. 'But she's trouble all the same. She's never satisfied with her own kind of people; she's always looking to hook some young man with money behind him.'

'She's got a dancer's legs,' the banker commented with a twinkle in his eye.

'Oh, spare me that, Ian,' Millie protested. 'I'd rather have a lighted stick of dynamite on my stage than Miss Greta Stacey!'

Dusk had fallen when Tess Fisher got word that Saul Banks, one of the young homesteaders, wanted to see him down at the fork of the arroyo. Tess could surmise what the homesteader had on his mind. Banks had brought Greta Stacey to the barbecue, but in the meantime she'd agreed to let Tess Fisher take her home. Greta had been giving Tess the eye for some time although she was also dating Saul Banks from time to time. Tess felt no jealousy towards his rival; Greta was simply an object of lust to the rancher's son. But he did intend to take advantage of her tonight, and no homesteader was going to stop him.

Tess turned and muttered a few words to a group of his father's cowhands who were standing by him protectively. When he was sure that they understood the situation he set off

jauntily for the arroyo rendezvous. As he walked his anger mounted towards the homesteaders who had the gall to summon a person of his status to such a sordid confrontation. He thought too of his sister, Blanche. He needed to have a word with his father about Blanche. She'd been quite shameless in dancing every dance with Charles Lynch.

Charles — or Carlos as Tess referred to him disparagingly because of his dark skin — was evidently of mixed race. He'd appeared on the scene the previous year and had set up a small-holding a stone's throw from the Fisher spread. There he supported himself quite easily because his needs were few. Blanche had taken a fancy to the tall, dark stranger, and Mrs Fisher also approved of the homesteader's quiet good manners whenever she and Blanche ran into him in town. To Will and Tess Fisher, however, he was just another of those parasites who blotted the fair landscape that they longed to own exclusively for themselves.

Saul Banks was patiently waiting for him at the water's edge, clearly visible by the light of the full moon. 'I hear you're taking Greta Stacey home tonight,' he said in a low, clear voice. He was four inches shorter than Tess and a good stone lighter, so Tess didn't fear him. Besides, the rancher's son knew that his father's men were not far behind him.

'That's right, Saul,' he sneered. 'She came with a boy, but she's going home with a man.'

The ferocity of the homesteader's attack took Tess Fisher by surprise. He drove the bigger man back with flailing fists. Blood began to spout from Fisher's nose and mouth, then a punch to the ribs brought him grunting to his knees. It seemed ages before his helpers turned up, causing Saul Banks to take a step backwards and reassess the situation.

'Kill him,' Tess urged them through his tears. 'Kill the filthy sonofabitch!'

Soberly, Tom Hall had noted the

exodus of the young men towards the arroyo. Sensing trouble he took his leave of a middle-aged townslady who had been demanding his attention. He was glad of the clear moonlight because the terrain was unfamiliar to him. He merely followed the excited voices ahead and watched his footing as he descended the slope.

When he caught sight of the mêlée in progress both in and around the arroyo, his heart sank. It was just like in the saloon. Would these hotheads never learn?

As he advanced a hand shot out and tore his shirt from his arm. Angrily the lawman turned and hit his assailant clean off his feet. There was a loud splash as the youngster landed flat on his back in the water.

Hall took another step towards the combatants, then froze. He was looking into the barrel of a revolver that was pointing at his stomach.

'Keep out of this, Marshal,' a voice warned him. 'You ain't in Anderton now.'

A shot rang out somewhere behind him and the revolver was whisked from the homesteader's hand as if by an invisible force.

'Aaah . . . ' The homesteader whined as he wrung his fingers in agony.

All eyes were turned on Mort Lazarus. The gunslinger surveyed them all almost contemptuously, his gun now reholstered as smoothly as he'd drawn it.

'Anyone looking for trouble had better ride out of here now,' he warned them coldly. 'Somebody's likely to get himself killed tonight, and it's not going to be me!'

6

Tom Hall sat at the window of the jailhouse and watched the folk pass by on their way to the large wooden church in the town centre. All the local dignitaries were dressed in style and seemed to have recovered from the festivities at Will Fisher's barbecue. Wisely the parson had rearranged the time of the service to allow everyone a lie-in, and it looked as if his thoughtfulness was going to be rewarded by a packed church.

Jo Deneuve was among the churchgoers, accompanied, of course, by the elegant Mort Lazarus. Lazarus almost had to fight off the many admirers who wanted him to relate how he'd saved the marshal's life the night before, and maybe prevented a bloodbath at Will Fisher's spread.

When the main street had emptied

Tom Hall settled down in his chair to read the *Anderton Gazette*, but the arrival of a group of riders outside the jail put an end to his repose.

A wiry, sunburnt man pushed his way through the door.

'I'm Alby Smith, Marshal,' he announced. 'I'm Mr Fisher's ranch foreman. You'd better come with us, and right away. There's been evil done on our land.'

Smith and the others rode tight-lipped and grim along the trail leading to the Fisher ranch-house. Whatever had happened had shocked even these men, who were hardened by a lifetime of struggle against the elements.

'It's past the ranch,' Smith informed the lawman. 'A little over two miles.'

They led the marshal down to the river where they had left a cowpoke standing at the water's edge, like a sentry.

There was no need for Alby Smith to explain the problem to Tom Hall. The

girl's body was spreadeagled in the mud, her clothing wrapped loosely around her.

'I asked the boys to dress her as well as they could,' the foreman said haltingly. 'It just didn't seem decent to leave her like she was.'

The lawman forced himself to look at the corpse. He'd only ever seen one dead woman before: his own mother. This girl had been very beautiful, though now her face was stained with blood from where her skull had been smashed in.

'Is she the girl they were fighting over last night?' Hall enquired.

'That's right,' Smith replied. 'Her name's Greta Stacey.'

'Well, we can't leave her here,' Hall said. 'Can we move her to the ranch-house until we can get word to her father and the undertaker?'

'And the judge,' Alby Smith reminded him.

'Yeah, of course, the judge,' the lawman said vaguely. 'She'll have to be told.'

It seemed ages before a wagon arrived from the ranch and the cowpokes managed to raise the body from its resting place. Burly fellers who'd have manhandled a male corpse like a side of beef were hesitant to lay hands on the dead girl's skin, as if they, too, were defiling her in some way.

They had hardly deposited their burden safely in the ranch-house when Will Fisher himself rode up, accompanied by Jo Deneuve and Mort Lazarus.

'Word got to us in church,' Fisher said. 'We came right away. It's terrible that it had to happen on my land!'

Meanwhile, Jo Deneuve was at her most businesslike. 'I'll need to examine the body,' she told the others.

'We brought her into the house,' Tom Hall said. 'She's in the next room.'

The girl's eyes narrowed, but she made no comment. She disappeared into the other room for a few minutes. When she came out she asked the marshal to drive her to where the body

had been discovered.

'I'll go with you,' Mort Lazarus offered, but the young judge declined courteously.

'There are things I need to discuss with Tom,' she said. 'This is a serious matter.'

Any pleasure the lawman might have derived from Mort's discomfiture vanished as he drove the buggy with Jo Deneuve at his side.

'You should never have moved the body,' she rebuked him. 'You may have destroyed vital clues.'

'The cowpokes had already moved it,' Hall defended himself lamely. 'She was half naked when they found her.'

'They are just cowboys,' she pointed out. 'You're the marshal and you're supposed to cooperate with the judge in a case like this.'

Tom felt like saying that he was only a lawman by default, but it didn't seem worth the effort. He realized now that he'd been stupid.

He halted the buggy at a point where

the river was accessible through the trees. They walked the fifty yards to the water's edge.

'I can see where they dragged her from the mud,' Jo commented. 'Were there many imprints when you first got here?'

'Sure. The cowhands had been stomping everywhere.'

The girl sighed. Nothing was going right. 'There are no large rocks here,' she said. 'So it couldn't have been an accidental fall.'

'Nope,' Tom Hall agreed. 'It took some force to cave her skull in like that. It wasn't no accident.'

'I wonder where the weapon is,' Jo mused.

'In the river,' Tom suggested. 'If he used a rock or a stick that would be the best way to get rid of it.'

The girl was moving about the muddy bank, oblivious to the state of her clothing. 'She wasn't killed here,' she decided after a while.

'You reckon?'

'There's no blood here,' Jo said. 'She'd stopped bleeding when she was left here.'

When they returned to the ranch-house, Alby Smith offered to take them to Jed Stacey's place. As it turned out, the bad news had preceded them and there were already neighbours assembled at the Stacey smallholding.

Jed Stacey, a tall, lumbering man was pacing the floor of his cabin, red-eyed and distressed. 'My little girl,' he repeated over and over again. 'Who'd want to kill my little girl?'

Tom Hall ushered the silent visitors outside to enable Jo Deneuve to commiserate with the grief-stricken father and also ask him some questions about his daughter.

'What were your thoughts when Greta failed to come home last night?' Jo enquired gently.

'I thought she must be staying with friends,' Stacey sobbed. 'I always told her not to risk riding after dark.'

'Did she go to the dance alone?'

'Nope. Saul Banks called for her. They've been friends ever since we moved here at the end of the war.'

'Was your wife still alive then?' Jo asked, more to appear friendly than because the question was relevant to the case.

'Yeah, but not for long,' Stacey replied. 'She was dead within two years; killed by hard work, I guess.'

'So your daughter wasn't born in these parts,' the young judge observed.

'Nope, in Dodge City,' the old man said. 'She was such a lovely baby. We . . . we both loved her so much.'

'What about Saul Banks?' Jo asked suddenly. 'Has he been here to see you today?'

Stacey shook his head. 'His father called over a little while ago,' he said. 'Saul was too upset to come. I suppose you heard about the fight he had with Tess Fisher and them fellers he calls his friends.'

'So Saul didn't bring Greta home last night?'

'Nope,' Stacey said bitterly. 'If you want to know what happened to my little girl, why don't you go ask Tess Fisher?'

7

If Tom Hall was looking forward to spending the rest of the day with Jo Deneuve he was quickly disappointed. The lady judge had other plans for the marshal. When they got back to the buggy she turned to the foreman.

'I'd be grateful if you'd lend Tom your horse, Mr Smith,' she told him. 'Then you can take me back to town. Tom can pick up his own horse at the ranch later on.'

'So what do you want me to do?' Tom Hall enquired.

'You can call on Saul Banks,' she answered. 'Get him to tell you everything he did from the time of the barbecue till noon today.'

Tom did some quick thinking; he didn't want another dressing down like the one she'd given him earlier.

'I ain't sure that my jurisdiction

reaches this far from town,' he objected.

She eyed him shrewdly. The marshal lacked experience and finesse, but she could read the honesty in his face. Back in Louisiana she'd met enough so-called pillars of society to recognize honesty as a rare and desirable quality in a man.

'I'm giving you the jurisdiction,' she told him. 'I suppose that if a U.S. marshal happens to ride along he'll take over from us. In the meantime it's you and I who represent justice in Anderton.'

Before the buggy drove away, Alby Smith gave the lawman directions to the Banks homestead, which was about five miles deeper into the hills. The day had warmed up and Tom didn't force Smith's grey gelding too quickly up the slopes. Besides, the mixture of colours on the mountains to the west was pleasing to his eyes. For the first time he felt at ease in his role as marshal. He'd be sorry when the election put an end to his short period of office and severed his relationship

51

with the beautiful Jo Deneuve, who was never far from his thoughts.

The homestead rested snugly in a hollow basin, dominated by an impressive wooded ridge. As he rode up to the house the front door opened and a short, slight man appeared. His cheeks were drawn and his breath laboured. Behind him Tom Hall could make out the figure of a woman, also short but fleshier.

The man viewed Hall's badge of office suspiciously and with a hostile glint in his eye. 'You're a long way from Anderton, Marshal,' he noted dryly. 'You lost or something?'

Tom Hall swung down easily from the saddle. 'Nope,' he grinned in friendly fashion. 'But I am thirsty.'

There was something about the stranger's smile that disarmed the woman in the doorway. 'You'd better come in then,' she told him. 'My husband will see to your horse.'

Inside, a youngster was sitting at the table, his face bruised and his eyes

bloodshot. He'd taken quite a beating at the barbecue.

Mrs Banks drew up a chair for the visitor. 'There's coffee made,' she told him. 'It'll only be a minute.'

Saul Banks and Tom Hall sat in silence for a few moments until a wheezing sound indicated that the old man was back in the house.

'Have you caught that young girl's killer yet?' Saul's father demanded. 'God, I cain't wait to see that varmint hanging from a tree!'

The lawman shook his head. 'That's why the judge sent me along, Mr Banks,' he replied. 'She wants me to ask Saul here a few questions.'

Mrs Banks reappeared at that moment, carrying a large pot of black coffee. 'Saul?' she said, placing the pot in the middle of the table. 'Why do you need to question Saul?'

Tom Hall could read the anxiety in her eyes. He felt sorry for her and hastened to reassure her.

'I'll have to question lots of folk, Mrs

53

Banks,' he said. 'That's what Miss Deneuve is doing right now in Anderton. We need to build up a picture of what went on last night.'

Saul Banks gave a sudden, short laugh. Until then he'd seemed to be in a dream. 'If she'd only gone home with me like she promised, she'd still be alive,' he reflected bitterly.

'But she didn't,' Tom prompted him. 'So what did you do, go home with your friends, the ones who took your side in the fight?'

'Nope, they all rode off before me,' Saul said. 'They'd seen enough when your friend Lazarus shot the gun out of Don Morgan's hand. They wanted me to go with them, but I hung about for Greta.'

'Then what happened?'

'She didn't want to talk to me,' Saul said. 'She was with Tess Fisher and his gang. When Tess took her back down to the river bank I knew I was just wasting my time, so I fetched my horse and rode back home.'

'Are you sure they went down to the river, just the two of them.'

Saul seemed to be wrestling with his conscience.

'Yep, I'm sure,' he answered. 'Fact is I followed them, but when I saw what they was up to I felt sick in my stomach.'

'Greta was no good for our Saul,' Mrs Banks said suddenly. 'I always knew that, but I didn't want the blame for poking my nose in. But I'll tell you one thing, Marshal: my boy never killed that girl. If I thought he had, I'd be the first person to turn him in to you!'

Tom Hall had almost reached Will Fisher territory when he heard shots away to the north. The gelding responded to his urging and soon he was galloping along a track that led him to an isolated cabin flanked by cotton-wood groves.

Tom dismounted and made his way cautiously to the cabin window and peeked in. It was empty. Then a small

flock of geese waddled up from the side of the building and made him start. They looked unconcerned by whatever had been going on in the vicinity.

The shooting started up again, very close at hand. Tom edged his way around the building, gun in hand.

A youngster was engaged in target practice in the yard at the back of the cabin. His targets were a row of tin cans on a wall some twenty yards away from him. He drew and sheathed his Colt anew for each shot. Tom Hall had met many men who were fast on the draw, and this youngster ranked with the best of them. His aim was good too, and each tin he aimed at duly hit the dust behind the stone wall.

'That was mighty fine shooting,' he complimented the young man when he'd finished firing, 'only now I got the drop on you.'

The homesteader turned and saw the badge on the lawman's shirt, and the friendly smile on his visitor's face.

'I always keep one slug in the barrel,' he said, but sheathed his gun all the same.

'This your place?' Hall asked, glancing around him.

'That's right. My name's Charles Lynch, but in Anderton they call me Carlos, because they think my mother's Mexican — which she is,' he added with a certain pride.

'Does she live with you?'

'No; she was in El Paso with my father, last time I heard.'

'That's a long way south,' Hall remarked.

'Further the better,' Lynch said. 'My father's a thief and a drunk. My mother asked me to go away before I ended up killing him.'

'Looks like you'd know how to,' the lawman said soberly. 'Specially with all that practising.'

Lynch shrugged his shoulders.

'I don't intend to kill anyone,' he replied. 'I got my love of guns from my father, but I didn't inherit his mean

streak. I need a gun to protect myself and my livestock, nothing else.'

'A young girl was murdered a mile or so from here last night,' Hall informed him.

'I know,' Lynch said. 'I was at the barbecue.'

'That's right, I remember you now,' the lawman said. 'You were with Will Fisher's daughter.'

'Blanche came on to me,' Lynch corrected him. 'I ain't the sort who can ask a girl like her for a dance or call on her at her home. Her father doesn't approve of fellers who breed geese and chickens.'

'Well, she seemed happy enough to be with you,' Tom remarked enviously, wishing that he had the same effect on Jo Deneuve.

'Yeah,' Charles agreed. 'Only, it won't get us anywhere. Her father and brother will see to that.'

He unsheathed his Colt and reloaded it. Tom Hall counted five shells entering the six-gun's chamber.

'What about Greta Stacey?' Hall prompted him.

'The lady judge called here with Will Fisher's foreman a couple of hours ago,' Lynch said with a level gaze. 'I told her everything I know about last night, but that's not much . . .'

★　★　★

Jo Deneuve sat in her office and pondered Greta Stacey's murder. It was a shame that most of the neutral characters in the drama — herself, Mort Lazarus, Ian Tanner, Miss Millie and Tom Hall — had left the barbecue not long after the trouble at the riverside.

There was a respectful knock at the door and the marshal came into the room. He'd seen the lamp burning in the window.

'Any luck, Tom?' she asked him.

'Not really. How about you?'

'I talked to Will Fisher earlier this evening. It looks as if Tess is in the

clear. He went to bed ill soon after the fight.'

'That's not what Saul Banks told me,' Hall said, and went on to recount the young homesteader's version of events. Jo Deneuve listened to him with considerable interest.

'I think I'll interview Tess Fisher first thing tomorrow,' she said when she'd finished.

'Will Fisher won't like that,' Tom said drily.

She looked up at him with a tired smile. 'If what you say is true,' she told him, 'his son isn't going to like it much either!'

8

Will Fisher almost choked over his bacon and eggs when the maid breezed into the drawing room and announced that Tess's presence was required in the judge's office as soon as possible.

'Who delivered the message?' the rancher demanded when he'd recovered from his coughing fit.

'The town marshal,' the maid replied. 'He was very polite about it.'

Tess was looking decidedly pale, and his mother gazed at him anxiously.

'Pull yourself together, son,' his father told him. 'Just repeat the story I gave Miss Deneuve last night. Do you want me to go with you?'

Tess shook his head. He felt like high-tailing it out of town.

'Well, finish your breakfast, dear,' Mrs Fisher urged her son soothingly.

'You'll feel much better on a full stomach.'

When the youngster had left the house Will Fisher decided to call on his friend Tim Riley at the Rockingstone Hotel. He found the saloon owner and Mort Lazarus seated at the same table; Riley was imbibing his first beer of the day while Lazarus was breakfasting on a hunk of bread and a bowl of white, sugared coffee.

'That goddam lady judge is like a dog with a bone,' Fisher complained to them. 'She's got my boy over at her office right now.'

Riley called for a clean glass and poured his visitor a shot of whiskey. He and the rancher shared several business interests and generally got on well together.

'Anything I can do for him, Will?' Riley enquired in his usual relaxed manner. 'Give him an alibi, maybe?'

'No, that's covered,' Fisher replied. 'He was with his mother and me all the time.'

Riley didn't blink an eye, though he knew the rancher was lying. Tess had been out of his parents' sight for most of the evening.

'It had to be one of the homesteaders who killed the girl,' Mort Lazarus chipped in suddenly.

Fisher turned to face him. 'Sure it was,' he agreed enthusiastically. 'But which one, and how are we going to prove it?'

'I've got plenty of time on my hands,' Lazarus told him. 'If you like, I can ride out to some of the homesteads and ask a few questions.'

'That was a homesteader you fired at,' Tim Riley reminded him.

'Sure it was,' Lazarus replied. 'But if I'd let him kill the marshal he'd be an outlaw now with a price on his head. I reckon I did the kid a favour . . . '

Meanwhile at the judge's office Tess Fisher was recounting the story his father had prepared for him. Jo Deneuve was seated opposite him across the desk while Tom Hall stood at

the window looking out onto the busy street.

'All right, Tess,' Jo sighed when he'd finished speaking. 'Now we're going to hear the version Saul Banks gave us of the night in question.'

Tess could feel his stomach turn over as the marshal repeated what Saul Banks had told him. Tess couldn't believe his bad luck. So Saul had been spying on him. What was the point of him sticking to a story that was so full of holes?

'Well, you heard the marshal,' Jo Deneuve said sharply. 'Who's lying, you or Saul?'

Tess thought quickly. What he lacked in moral fibre he made up for in animal cunning.

'Who else is backing Saul's story?' he asked aggressively.

'Nobody — so far,' Jo Deneuve said. 'It's just your word against his.'

The master-stroke came to Tess in a flash. 'I been lying to you,' he said unexpectedly. 'I did go down to the

river with Greta Stacey.'

Jo Deneuve's spirits rose; at last they were getting somewhere. 'You did?' she asked.

'Sure I did,' Tess confirmed. 'She asked me to go with her. She wanted me to . . . ' He hesitated as if he was afraid to speak too frankly in front of a lady. 'Trouble was I was too badly hurt after the fight with Saul. I . . . I just wasn't any use to her.'

'So you left her there and went back to the barbecue?' Tom Hall asked.

'Yeah, but only after Saul Banks came steaming up and started yelling at Greta,' Tess said.

'What did he yell?' Jo Deneuve enquired.

Tess lowered his gaze. 'I oughtn't to say,' he said humbly. 'He was just mad. He likely didn't mean it.'

'What did he say?' Tom Hall demanded, raising his voice.

'He said that if he couldn't have her, nobody would,' Tess mumbled. 'Then he ran off.'

'And that was the last time you saw Greta?' Joe asked.

'That's right,' Tess confirmed. 'I'd had enough of them both by then. I'd seen how vicious Saul could be, and I couldn't face fighting him again. I was just glad to get back safely to the ranch, and that's where I stayed.'

9

Crazy Jack grew more and more agitated as he tried to answer the questions the lawman and the young lady judge threw at him.

Jack was by no means crazy, but he was no longer young and an illness in middle-age had robbed him of his power of speech. It had paralysed him, too, for a short while but gradually his strength came back and he continued to eke out a living growing vegetables and hunting for small game in the woodlands and adjacent hills.

Jack was impressed by the young lady; she was attractive, beautiful even, and she rode stylishly as if she'd received proper schooling in horsemanship. She was sharp, too, sharp as a tack. She did her best to understand what Jack was trying to express and it saddened the old man to think that she

probably took him for a fool like the rest.

The problem was that Jack had never learned reading and writing. Now he attempted to draw figures with a stick in the dusty ground in front of his cabin. He drew figures to represent horsemen and a moon to show that they rode only at night. He'd heard them pass in the distance, on their way to and from the hills. He took them to be strangers, since there was no call for local folk to be abroad at such a time.

The lawman seemed a good sort, not as sharp as the girl but solid and dependable, the kind of man who'd face heavy odds if his cause was just. Unfortunately, the marshal could make no more sense of his drawings than the girl could. They both shook their heads in despair; the old feller knew nothing.

But Mad Jack did know that another man was asking questions of his neighbours. The man was tall and rangy and wore a pair of fancy shooters he looked like he could use. His speech

was smooth and mild as he won the homesteaders' confidence by telling them that he was sure the young girl had been killed by one of the townsfolk. The homesteaders listened to the stranger's sweet talk and told one another that he was on their side. But Mad Jack could read the killer instinct in Mort Lazarus' eyes and whenever the man's name was mentioned in his presence the old man would express his disapproval by spitting into the dust.

The nightriders were no figment of the dumb homesteader's imagination. By day they rested concealed deep in the hills; by moonlight they familiarized themselves with the layout of the land as far as Will Fisher's spread. Occasionally one or two of the cowpokes thought they heard hooves in the distance as they watched the herd or lay snugly in sleeping-bags under the prairie sky, but the sound didn't worry them unduly since nothing seemed to be amiss and the peace of the range remained undisturbed.

Then one night as three of Fisher's cowhands, Wiloughby, Davies and Brewer, made coffee around a campfire on the remotest corner of the spread, the sound of riders was heard again.

'There they go again,' Wiloughby commented. 'Can you hear them this time?'

His two companions could not suppress their smiles. So far only Wiloughby, the oldest hand among them, had heard the mystery horses, and they'd ribbed him unmercifully over it.

'Sure I hear them,' Davies grinned. 'Them's ghost riders — dead Indian braves searching for that old happy hunting ground in the sky!'

Suddenly Brewer stopped smiling.

'Whatever it is, it's stirring up the herd,' he said, jumping to his feet. 'I'm gonna take a look.'

His companions were not far behind him. Leaping into their saddles they began to fan out to cover as great an area as possible. Wiloughby took a deep

breath at what he could make out in the distance. A huge section of the herd was on the move.

'Stampede!' he yelled to the others. 'They're headed towards the homesteads. You two head them off.'

He watched them ride away. There was no point in following them, since there was still the remainder of the cows to think about. The experienced cowhand was puzzled; he couldn't believe the stampede had been started deliberately. There was no reason for the homesteaders to stampede their neighbour's cattle towards their own homes. It was sheer madness.

Meanwhile, Davies and Brewer were riding alongside the flank of the herd, whooping and yelling and trying to divert the steers back onto Fisher's spread. Suddenly Davies noticed another rider over to his left. He heard two sharp cracks and saw his friend, Brewer, fall forward onto his mount's neck. Davies realized they were being fired on, and hastily drew his own Colt

from its holster.

Wiloughby heard the shots in the distance but still held back. Those crazy youngsters, Davies and Brewer, must be firing their guns in the air. That would only scare the cattle even further, he thought.

The shooting continued and that worried him. He decided to go back and stoke up the fire so that his pardners would have a beacon to guide them back to base.

He heaved a sigh of relief when he reached the fire. There were men there already, helping themselves to the coffee which had been brewing. Some of the ranch-hands must have been passing by. Alby Smith, the foreman, was renowned for his ability to sense trouble even before it happened.

'Alby?' Wiloughby called out as he dismounted.

One of the men stood up and faced him. It wasn't Alby Smith but a swarthy, heavily moustached feller who was a total stranger to him.

'Welcome,' Wiloughby said ironically. 'Why don't you boys help yourselves to some coffee?'

'We already did, *Señor*,' the swarthy man replied. Then he drew his gun smoothly from its holster and shot the cowhand twice in the stomach.

10

It wasn't until the afternoon of the next day that news of the killings reached the township of Anderton. Will Fisher was in the Rockingstone Hotel with his son Tess, engaged in a game of cards for friendly stakes with Tim Riley and Mort Lazarus.

Will Fisher would not normally be seen wasting his time playing cards this early in the day. He was more likely to be counting his profits from his ranching and other pursuits and scheming how to increase them still further.

But recently the rancher had been courting the friendship of the gunslinger Lazarus, who had proved his mettle on the night of the barbecue. Although the lady judge and the town marshal were spreading their murder inquiry throughout the territory, Will Fisher was uncomfortably aware that

his son Tess was still a prime suspect in the eyes of many people, including some who called themselves friends.

Fisher knew that the homesteaders were seething over the death of Jed Stacey's daughter, and he also knew that many of them had a volatile nature. If they thought they could prove anything against Tess, they were quite capable of taking the law into their own hands.

Tom Hall was settling in quickly to his role as the town marshal, and was gaining daily in competence and confidence. Nevertheless, Will Fisher doubted Hall's ability to quell a serious disturbance such as a riot or a lynch mob. Lazarus, on the other hand, was obviously a man who had lived by the gun. If anyone could look after Tess it was Mort Lazarus, and the rancher was prepared to pay handsomely for that protection if it became necessary.

The saloon door swung open as Tim Riley was dealing a fresh hand of cards. Will Fisher looked up and saw his

75

ranch foreman, Alby Smith, hurrying towards their table. The cowpoke's face was sweat-stained and grim, and Fisher realized at once that something serious had happened. He dropped his cards face-downwards on the table.

'What's wrong, Alby?' he enquired. 'You look all het up.'

There was a vacant chair at the table, but the ranch foreman was too agitated to sit down.

'There's been killing on the range,' he blurted out. 'We've lost three good men.'

Will Fisher sucked in air. He was conscious of his prominent position in the territory. Who'd be crazy enough to attack his cowhands?

'Tell me what happened?' he said.

The bartender hurried over with a drink for the newcomer, but Smith waved him away.

'Wiloughby, Brewer and Davies were camped out at Indian Creek,' he explained. 'We had a lot of cattle gathered in the creek and they needed

watching. Somebody went and stampeded them — I've got all the hands out rounding them up. Davies and Brewer must have taken up the chase. Anyways, they ran into bigger trouble than they could handle. We found their bodies this morning; they'd both been shot and Davies must have been dragged along by his horse because half his face was torn away when we found him.'

'What about Wiloughby?' Fisher asked. 'You said we lost three men.'

Smith nodded, but could hardly continue. Wiloughby had been a personal friend; both men were from Wyoming and they'd both worked other spreads together before joining Fisher's ranch on the same day.

'Wiloughby stayed behind,' he said. 'But they got him all the same. No doubt the campfire attracted them. He got it in the stomach. I only hope it didn't take him too long to die. He didn't even have a chance to draw his gun, but at least Davies and Brewer got

a few shots off, though it don't look like they killed anyone.'

'Where were they driving the cows?' Fisher demanded.

'Nowhere in particular,' Smith replied awkwardly. 'Most of them are spread out amongst the homesteads.'

'The homesteads . . . ' Will Fisher's eyes narrowed. He turned his gaze on Mort Lazarus who was listening attentively.

'What's your opinion, Mort?' he asked.

Lazarus weighed up the question thoughtfully.

'Like I told you, Mr Fisher,' he replied respectfully. 'The homesteaders don't reckon that the Stacey girl was killed by one of their own kind. They're looking to place the blame elsewhere.'

Tess Fisher squirmed in his seat as the gunslinger spoke. Tess knew that his name was mud outside of Anderton, and even in the township there were folk who no longer greeted him when they met.

Will Fisher's face was stony; he

wasn't going to be harassed by a gaggle of squatters.

'Tell the boys to keep rounding the cows up,' he told Smith. 'And tell them to be hard on any homesteaders that are harbouring our cattle.'

'They're not harbouring them,' Mr Fisher,' Smith objected. 'Fact is, our cattle are grazing on their land.'

'I don't recognize their land,' Fisher rebuked him sharply. 'I want their corrals flattened and their crops trampled. Do you understand?'

'Sure, I understand, Mr Fisher,' the foreman replied wearily.

'And I want the varmints who killed my men,' Fisher added angrily. 'And when I catch them, you can tell those homesteaders that I'll string them up in public so that all their family and children can watch them hang!'

11

Ian Tanner was sufficiently concerned about the general situation to take time off from his banking activities and call on Tom Hall over at the jailhouse.

'Things are getting pretty tense out there on the homesteads, Tom,' the banker said, accepting the lawman's offer to sit down and make himself comfortable.

'So I hear,' Hall replied. 'Seems like Fisher's cowpokes have been heavy-handed with the settlers.'

'They're under orders from Fisher himself,' Tanner said. 'Not that they needed much prodding. They all lost good friends the other night, though why they're blaming the homesteaders is beyond my understanding. Could have been anyone stirring them cattle up.'

'It's all down to the girl's murder,'

Hall suggested. 'The settlers reckon she was killed by one of Fisher's cowhands or a young buck from Anderton. They just don't accept that one of her own kind could have done it.'

The banker shook his head sadly. 'It's got to be sorted out,' he mused. 'The homesteaders don't come into Anderton like they used to. The shops are losing trade. Even Miss Millie's place is suffering. On dancing nights the Golden Fleece is half empty. Granted that the homesteaders are trouble from time to time, but Anderton's always been the place where they've spent their spare dollars.'

'What about the bank?' the marshal enquired. 'Are you losing custom?'

'Not thus far,' Tanner replied. 'Most of my customers live here in town. It's not that the homesteaders are poor, but they are old-fashioned and they're as likely to stuff money into an old mattress as deposit it sensibly in a bank. Still, if there's less money circulating in the shops, the banking

business is bound to feel the cold sooner or later.'

'My pa always kept his money hid in a mattress,' Tom Hall said. 'Till the bedroom caught fire one night.'

'That was bad luck,' Tanner sympathized. 'Did he lose much?'

'Nope,' Hall grinned. 'He never did believe in paper money. Kept it all in coins!'

'Of course, banks can let you down as well,' Tanner observed seriously. 'Bad investments, a crooked cashier, maybe a robbery even.'

'Nothing like that ever happened to you, Mr Tanner?' the lawman enquired.

The banker shook his head emphatically. 'Nope; my staff are very loyal and I've known them a long time,' he said. 'My security's good; nobody could get into my safe without a fight.'

'I've seen your cashiers,' Tom Hall remarked drily. 'They're both pretty long in the tooth.'

His observation seemed to amuse the

banker. 'You reckon I should employ younger men?' he enquired with a chuckle.

'Why not?' the marshal said. 'Fellers who can handle themselves.'

'Do you know the difference between a cashier of twenty and a cashier of fifty?' Tanner asked.

'Go on, you tell me,' Tom said, noting the twinkle in the banker's eye.

'In a shoot-out, your young feller of twenty is risking thirty years of life more than my fifty-year-old cashiers.'

Tom Hall sat there, thinking it over.

'Besides which,' the banker went on triumphantly. 'If the bank gets robbed and put out of business, the young feller still has the time and opportunity to move onto another job, whereas my employees' futures depend entirely on the bank they work in.'

'OK,' Tom smiled. 'You've convinced me. When I get to the age of fifty I'm gonna call on you and ask you for a job. If you and your bank

are still around, that is!'

Ian Tanner's eyes had strayed to the loose sheets of paper on the desk in front of the town marshal.

'You expected to do much paperwork in your spare time?' he asked.

Hall shoved the papers to one side. 'It's Jo Deneuve's idea,' he informed his visitor. 'It's a list of the folk we've talked to about Greta Stacey's death, and some of the answers they've given us.'

'That's mighty thorough of her,' Tanner commented approvingly.

'Yeah,' Tom agreed. 'Jo's particularly interested in anyone who happened to be in Dodge City while the Staceys were living there.'

Tanner stared at him. 'Why's that?' he asked.

'It's got to do with something Jo calls motive,' the lawman explained. 'She's wondering if anybody has a grudge against the Staceys that goes back to the old days in Dodge.'

'Any luck so far?' the banker asked.

Tom Hall shook his head. 'Not so far,' he admitted. 'Only one or two who may have passed through Dodge on their way elsewheres. But we're still trying.'

12

Mort Lazarus smiled at his guest as he poured her a glass of wine from the bottle that had been chilling in an ice-bucket since sundown. The bottle, and the ice-bucket, had been thoughtfully provided by Tim Riley, proprietor of Anderton's Rockingstone Hotel.

Lazarus and Jo Deneuve were partaking of the meal in a secluded corner of the hotel dining-room. The place was tranquil since all the other diners had finished their meals and departed, some to the privacy of their bedrooms and others to the tumult of the gaming tables in Riley's saloon bar.

'Riley was boasting to me about the quality of his wines,' Lazarus told the girl. 'So I decided to put him to the test. Well, what do you think of it?'

The lady judge sipped the white

liquid then replaced her glass on the table.

'It's fine,' she said. 'And it's not too sweet for me.'

'Sounds like you're a real expert,' Lazarus mocked her gently.

'I lived in France for a time,' Jo reminded him in a matter-of-fact tone. 'We usually drank wine with our meals.'

'Does that mean that this evening isn't a treat for you?' Lazarus said.

The judge hastened to reassure her host.

'Not at all,' she said. 'It's always a treat for a girl to be invited to dinner. By the way, what's the occasion, Mort?'

He raised his glass in a smooth movement. All his movements were smooth, like a cougar.

'I'd say it was my birthday,' he teased her. 'Only then you'd ask me my age, and that's something I can't reveal to a beautiful young lady such as yourself.'

She managed to avert her gaze. The man's eyes were deep, almost hypnotic.

She found Mort Lazarus very attractive, yet something inside her told her to beware of him and not fall under his spell.

'I don't really know much about you at all,' she countered. 'Though you've been very kind to me since I've been in Anderton.'

'Since *we've* been in Anderton,' Lazarus said. 'Fate threw us together on the stage, remember?'

She nodded in agreement, but was not distracted from her theme.

'For instance,' she went on. 'I don't even know what kind of work you do.'

He spread his hands wide — pale, slim, elegant hands that would be equally at home dealing an ace from the bottom of the pack, or thumbing the hammer of a Colt .45.

'You've asked me that before,' he said.

She smiled to put him at his ease. Women have their guiles, too.

'All that I can remember is a long list that I forgot to write down,' she told

him. 'I mean your real profession.'

'Speculator,' Lazarus replied. 'I assess a given situation and try to profit from it.'

'That's fine,' Jo said, taking another sip of wine. 'But why Anderton?'

Lazarus shrugged his shoulders. 'I don't know,' he answered. 'Maybe I'm just resting.'

Jo Deneuve concealed her impatience, though she'd have loved to know the answer to her question.

'Well, you're hardly resting, Mort,' she commented casually. 'You've been just as active out on the homesteads as the marshal and I have.'

Lazarus sank back in his chair, and eyed the girl with amusement.

'So that's it,' he said. 'I've been treading on the marshal's corns and he's gone running to you about it.'

Jo felt a flush rise to her cheeks, not for herself but for Tom Hall.

'Tom hasn't even mentioned it to me,' she protested. 'I'm merely curious as to your motives, that's all.'

Lazarus could see that he'd come close to angering his guest, which was not what he wanted at present.

'I'd like to know the truth about the girl's death,' he said earnestly. 'And so would Will Fisher. He wants the heat taken off his son Tess.'

'I didn't realize there was any heat on Tess,' the judge replied coolly. 'After all, there were scores of people at the barbecue.'

'But not that many with a reason to kill Greta Stacey,' Lazarus countered. 'Have you narrowed the field down at all?'

Jo Deneuve shook her head. 'Not as much as I'd like,' she admitted. 'Have you found out anything?'

'No more than I knew at the start,' Lazarus said. 'But that's more than enough.'

She stared at him. 'Well, what is it?' she demanded.

'Saul Banks is your killer,' Lazarus said. 'And if I was marshal of Anderton Saul would be kicking his heels in the

jailhouse already.'

'Really, Mort,' the girl rebuked him. 'You can't say things like that without proof.'

Lazarus reached out suddenly and gripped her wrist like a vice.

'You should order Saul Banks' arrest right away,' he told her vehemently. 'Otherwise you may have a lot more deaths on your hands.'

13

Tess Fisher sat opposite Mort Lazarus in the latter's hotel room, and hung on every word the gunslinger said.

'I don't care what the lady judge and the town marshal think,' Lazarus told him. 'I figure it was Saul Banks who killed the girl.'

'There ain't no proof, Mort,' Tess said. 'They been questioning everybody, yet they ain't found no proof against Saul.'

'There's no proof against you, Tess,' Lazarus reminded him. 'But all the homesteaders reckon that you're guilty.'

Tess felt a shiver run along his spine. He'd been living on his nerves since Greta Stacey's death, fearing a bullet from an avenging settler's gun.

'Well, I didn't kill her,' he whined. 'I don't reckon I could kill anybody, Mort.'

Lazarus managed to conceal the contempt he felt for the spoilt brat in front of him. 'We've got to get Saul Banks to confess,' Lazarus said.

'How do we do that?' Tess asked. 'He ain't gonna change his story.'

'I reckon I might just make him,' the gunslinger smiled coldly.

Tess Fisher's eyes filled with hope. 'Why don't you, Mort?' he urged him. 'Pa would give you anything you wanted.'

'I'll need a witness,' Lazarus said. 'My word won't be enough unless there's someone backing it up.'

'Well, take someone along with you,' Tess advised him.

'That's the idea, Tess,' Lazarus replied. 'I want you along there as well.'

Tess gave it some thought. He didn't really want to get involved, but he could think of no way out.

'What about Saul?' he asked. 'How you gonna made him talk to us?'

'That's easy,' Lazarus said. 'I'll tell him the same story I just told you.

Only, in the new version it'll be you who's gonna make the confession . . . '

Tess Fisher hardly slept for the next couple of nights in anticipation of the adventure Mort Lazarus had promised him. By the third morning he'd had no word from the gunslinger, but that very silence told him that he was to leave Anderton before noon, as had been arranged.

He told nobody about the plan, not even his father, since the gunslinger had warned him that any mention of the intended meeting with Saul Banks might invalidate any confession the young homesteader made.

Another reason for Tess Fisher's growing excitement was that Mort had indicated that he was ready to use force to exact a confession from Saul. He remembered the beating Saul had given him. Well, now the reckoning was at hand.

He remained vigilant as he rode through the open countryside; he didn't want to make a target for a squatter's

rifle. It angered him that he should be suspected of the girl's death — him, the son of Anderton's richest citizen. As if he'd soil his hands on a whore like Greta Stacey.

He was ten miles out of Anderton when he turned at the river confluence and followed the tributary stream into Acorn Creek. The creek narrowed rapidly and there was no strong trail to speak of, so he kept his mount as close as possible to the water's edge until he'd covered the half-mile or so to the spot where Mort Lazarus was waiting for him.

Tess dismounted and allowed his horse to wander over to where the other animal was grazing. Although Tess was as tall as Lazarus and better built, he always felt awed by the gunslinger's presence. He'd expected to find two men waiting for him; he was frankly puzzled by the situation, but felt almost too shy to air his concern.

'What about Saul?' he asked awkwardly. 'Is he on his way?'

Lazarus shook his head, but didn't look at all concerned. For a brief moment Tess had the joyous thought that maybe he'd killed Saul already.

'Nope, he ain't coming,' Lazarus informed him. 'He decided to go to Devil's Canyon instead.'

'Devil's Canyon? But that's nowhere near here,' Tess objected. 'It ain't near nowhere.'

'That's right,' the gunslinger agreed. 'Maybe that's why it attracted him. When I told him how high feelings are running against him and the other settlers, he thought he'd better go look for a good defensive position in case things turn out for the worst.'

Tess allowed himself a little smile. Lazarus must be thinking the same thing as he was.

'All there is in Devil's Canyon is water,' he said. 'If they don't carry supplies we can starve them out.'

The gunslinger's gaze seemed distant.

'I warned him of that,' he said. 'Him and his friends are stocking up.'

The smile vanished from Tess Fisher's face. 'You warned him! Whose side are you on, Mort?'

Lazarus shrugged his shoulders. 'I guess I'm a changeable kind of feller, Tess,' he said. 'When I'm in Anderton I side with your father and the rest of the townsfolk. When I'm out here I kinda lean towards the homesteaders.'

Tess felt suddenly alone and vulnerable; he felt a cold shiver run through his body. But despite his fear, the youngster's cunning didn't desert him. He must do nothing to upset or provoke Lazarus in the strange mood the gunslinger was in.

'I guess I trust you, Mort,' he said with a forced grin. 'You know what you're doing. If you stick by my pa, he'll make you a rich man.'

Mort crouched down and let the fingers of his right hand dangle in the cool water of the creek.

'I'm gonna be rich with or without your pa, Tess,' he said seriously. He was looking away now, as if something had

caught his notice on the far bank; Tess knew he had to take control of the situation. His companion's talk was crazy. Tess went for his gun.

It hadn't cleared the holster when he found himself staring into the barrel of Lazarus' Colt .45.

'You'd better get out of here,' Lazarus told him. 'Before I lose my temper.'

'I didn't mean nothing, Mort,' Tess babbled, the sweat running down his face. 'I was scared, that's all.'

'Get going,' Lazarus hissed. 'Now!'

Tess Fisher turned away and stumbled towards his horse. Before he'd reached it, Lazarus had shot him three times in the back.

14

Tom Hall called in at the bank in the course of his noon patrol of Anderton. He liked to show the townsfolk that the marshal they employed did not spend all his time dozing in his office chair.

As he reached the steps of the bank he saw Tess Fisher ride by on his way out of town. True to form the rancher's son didn't even acknowledge the lawman's presence on the sidewalk. As far as he and his father were concerned the temporary marshal was Ian Tanner's choice, a choice that they intended to overturn at the next council meeting.

'Come on in, Marshal,' the banker's voice boomed as Hall entered the cool interior of the building. 'I take it you want to open a deposit account with us.'

The two white-haired, walrus-moustached tellers looked up from

their accounts and gave the newcomer a brief glance. The two men were friendly in a gruff sort of way, but Tom Hall just couldn't figure them out. If they'd always been bank clerks, why hadn't they settled down in their own territory and raised families there?

The lawman grinned ruefully at the banker, who was making a great show of opening a leather-bound ledger on a fresh page.

'Hold your horses, Mr Tanner,' he said. 'So far my wages only just cover my debts.'

Tanner closed the ledger smartly and stashed it under the counter.

'Never mind, Tom,' he said soothingly. 'Who knows, maybe you've got a glittering future in the world of law and order. You could put up for county sheriff one day, or make U.S. marshal. On the other hand you may prefer to lay down your guns and opt for the judiciary. A federal judge must earn a fortune the way crime is going in this fair land we call America.'

Tom Hall knew when his leg was being pulled, and he replied cheerfully.

'I guess that sort of thing is more in Jo Deneuve's line,' he said. He half-turned and glanced across the street at Tudball's hardware store. 'Now that's something I could go into,' he mused aloud. 'A little place I could build up as the township expanded.'

Tanner came round the counter and put a hand on the lawman's shoulder.

'Don't let Tudball hear you talking like that, Tom,' he said. 'He's a leading member of the town council. If you get on his wrong side he'll run you out of town on the end of a pitchfork!'

Tom Hall smiled at the remark, but his smile was tinged with bitterness. He knew that he hadn't earned the respect of the townsfolk, many of whom shared Will Fisher's opinion of their stop-gap marshal. Before he had time to reply he heard Joel's voice calling him from the doorway.

'The lady judge wants to see you, Marshal,' the big man informed him.

101

'She's over in her office.'

The windows of Jo Deneuve's office were open to let some cool air in, but when the lawman presented himself she asked him to close them so that they could talk in strict privacy.

With the sounds of the street blotted out, she motioned him to sit down on the opposite side of the desk.

'I've had a reply from Dodge City,' she told him.

Tom Hall waited in silence for her to explain.

'A week ago,' she said, 'I wired the marshal's office in Dodge and asked for any information they might have on the Stacey family. This is the reply they sent me.'

She pushed a sheet of paper across the table. He picked it up and read: Jed Stacey — record of physical violence. Wife, May Stacey, and daughter Greta (adopted, age 8, July 1860).

'What I don't like,' Jo Deneuve told him, 'is that Jed Stacey spoke to me about his daughter as a baby.'

Tom Hall scratched his cheek thoughtfully. 'He could have known her for years before they adopted her,' he pointed out.

'Or he could have been lying to me,' Jo countered.

'What if he was?' Tom said. 'He was mighty upset when we spoke to him. Maybe he wasn't thinking straight.'

The young lady judge remained unconvinced. 'I'm going out to Jed's place,' she said. 'I need to sort this out.'

'Who's going with you?' the lawman asked. 'Lazarus?'

She turned and stared at him. He sounded almost bitter.

'I was about to ask you, Tom,' she said. 'That's if you're free.'

'I'm free,' he assured her. 'I'll go saddle some horses.'

About five miles outside of Anderton they met Saul Banks' parents driving towards them on a buckboard.

'We're on our way into town for the weekly supplies,' Mrs Banks volunteered. Her husband coughed and wheezed at

her side. The effort of halting the horses had proved almost too much for him.

'And we're heading the opposite way,' Jo Deneuve said sociably.

'You're not going to see Saul?' Mrs Banks enquired. Her voice betrayed the same anxiety as when she'd served up coffee back at the homestead.

'Nope, not Saul,' the marshal assured her. 'We're on our way to see Jed Stacey.'

The older couple exchanged meaningful glances.

'What's wrong?' Jo Deneuve asked. 'Is Jed ill or something?'

'Not ill, exactly,' Banks said. 'But he ain't hisself either. Since Greta's gone he's taken to locking his door and yelling at visitors to go away.'

Tom Hall and Jo Deneuve rode the rest of the way in silence. When they reached the Stacey homestead they dismounted at the side of the barn and let the horses water at a nearby trough. They'd only walked a few yards when Jed Stacey's voice challenged them

from the open window of his shack.

'What do you two want?' he demanded angrily. 'I'm fed up with questions and sly glances and folk talking about me and my little girl behind my back.'

Tom Hall felt vulnerable in the open yard, but his companion seemed unconcerned.

'I need to check out your story, Mr Stacey,' she said in a clear voice. 'Such as why you didn't tell me Greta was adopted, not as a baby but as an eight-year-old child?'

Luckily, the lawman at her side was concentrating very much on the present rather than on events before the Civil War. Tom Hall saw a glint of metal in the window and he unceremoniously dragged the young judge down to ground level as the rifle shot splintered the barn wall behind them.

'She always was my baby, my little girl,' Jed screamed. 'When her mother died I looked after her; I even took her into my own bed. She swore she'd

never leave me. That was before she turned into a slut and let herself be laid by all the farmhands. And then she got tired of them, too, and gave herself to that Fisher boy, the sonofabitch!'

'Did you kill her, Jed?' Tom Hall called out.

'Sure I did. I killed her right here and then I took her back to where Tess Fisher had defiled her. She boasted to me about it, Marshal, and she was my little girl!'

Jo Deneuve moved her head to one side and glanced at the lawman. His face was white. She wondered if it was with fear or anger, or a mixture of the two.

The rifle sang out again, and this time Tom Hall snapped off a shot of his own. Before the girl knew what was happening, the lawman was on his feet and zig-zagging towards the cabin. Jo tried to shout a warning but the words stuck in her throat. She heard the crash as he kicked the cabin door in and disappeared inside. Then there was one final, muffled explosion.

'Tom . . . Oh, my God!'

Oblivious to the danger she sprang to her feet and ran to the shack. At the doorway she took a deep breath. Tom Hall was standing over the prone body of the homesteader, shielding her from the ugliness of the scene.

'You, you killed him, Tom?' she stammered.

He turned and walked towards her.

'No,' he said. 'He jammed the barrel under his chin and pulled the trigger.'

Suddenly she felt light-headed and she sagged against the wall. Tom reached out and held her steady. The colour had drained from her cheeks.

'I've never been so scared,' she told him.

'That's natural,' he said gently. 'You could have been killed back there.'

Then the tears broke and she was no longer a judge but a vulnerable young woman.

'You fool, Tom,' she said fiercely. 'I wasn't scared for me. I was scared for you . . . '

15

If the judge and the town marshal were hoping that Jed Stacey's confession would reduce the tension around Anderton, their hopes were short-lived. At ten o'clock the following morning rancher Will Fisher strode into the jailhouse and announced that his son Tess had not been seen since the previous day.

'I saw him ride out of town yesterday at noon,' Tom Hall remarked.

'You and a dozen others,' the rancher said impatiently. 'And I'm telling you that my boy ain't been seen since.'

'What about the ranch?' the lawman enquired. 'Maybe he's camping out someplace with some of your cow-hands.'

Will Fisher slumped down onto a chair. He'd aged visibly overnight. 'My foreman Alby Smith is scouring the

countryside,' he said. 'Only I don't hold out much hope in that direction. Tess ain't the sort who wants to rough it out on the range. Besides . . . '

'Besides what?' Tom Hall prompted him. Although he had no reason to like the rancher, he could sympathize with his plight. He thought, too, of the rancher's wife and daughter. He could imagine what they must be going through.

'I lost three good men out on the range the other night,' Fisher said. 'I reckon they were shot by the homesteaders, only I ain't got no proof. But I'm telling you straight, Marshal, God help them if they've done anything to my son!'

He stood up abruptly, unwilling to betray his emotions to the lawman.

'I want you to do everything you can to find him, Marshal,' he said. 'In fact, I'm ordering you to do everything you can.'

The first thing Tom Hall did was call at Jo Deneuve's office to see if the

young judge would apply her logical mind to this new problem.

'Well, if Will Fisher's hands are searching his land you'll simply be wasting time covering the same ground,' she pointed out. 'You need to recruit bands of volunteers who'll ride from dawn to dusk, and they'll need to be given a distinct section of territory to cover each time they ride out.'

Tom Hall scratched his chin dubiously.

'I cain't see the townsfolk flocking to join me,' he said honestly.

'Don't underestimate yourself, Tom,' she told him. 'You've just helped me clear up a murder that was threatening to split the whole region. Besides, the search isn't all down to you. You'll have to talk to men like Ian Tanner at the bank, Tim Riley at the Rockingstone Hotel and shopkeepers like Mr Tudball opposite. They're all members of the town council and it's up to them to call for volunteers.'

'What about me?' he asked. 'I cain't be everywhere at once.'

'You're right,' she said. 'Your role will be to visit the homesteads. The homesteaders don't like the townsfolk and vice versa. You've got to keep them apart, Tom; at least until Tess Fisher shows up.'

Tom Hall nodded his head in agreement, but at the back of his mind there lurked the suspicion that they'd solved the Greta Stacey murder a day too late — and that maybe Tess Fisher was not going to turn up alive.

★ ★ ★

Despite the continuing search for Tess Fisher, Ian Tanner decided against postponing the soirée he'd arranged to celebrate the fifth anniversary of his bank in Anderton.

Of course, the Fishers made it clear that they were not in the right frame of mind to attend a social event at this time. However, they were allowing their daughter, Blanche to represent them, since they felt it would do her good to

get away from the anxious, oppressive atmosphere of the house, if only for a few hours.

To everybody's surprise, Blanche came into the banker's drawing room accompanied by the young home-steader Charles Lynch, or Carlos as the young bucks of Anderton referred to him disparagingly.

Charles had been taken completely by surprise by the invitation which Blanche gave him about a week previous to her brother's disappearance.

'Please come, Charles,' she begged him when she saw him hesitate. 'I really won't enjoy myself if you're not there.'

'I just don't know, Blanche,' he replied, shaking his head. 'I ain't ever been to that sort of thing. Besides, your folks are going to be there, and you know how your pa feels about me.'

'My father neither likes nor dislikes you, Charles,' she tried to assure him. 'He doesn't really know you. But my mother has often met you here in town, and she thinks you're very nice.'

Charles Lynch didn't have the heart to refuse her, though he had serious forebodings about the evening. Blanche was a pretty girl, lively and wealthy. She could take her pick of Anderton's young men, yet she'd chosen him as her beau. It didn't make sense and he feared that one day she'd come to her senses and turn from him. In the meantime, all he could do was purchase a new shirt and pants and hope that he wouldn't look and feel too out of place among the dignitaries of the township.

He decided to ride into Anderton unarmed. Although he kept a weapon close at hand at all times on the homestead, he realized that he was likely to offend some of the other guests if he arrived at the banker's home toting a gun.

When Charles and Blanche entered the large drawing room, Miss Millie, who was co-hosting the soirée, hurried over to greet the young homesteader and put him at his ease.

'We're so glad you could come, Charles,'

113

she said when Blanche proudly presented him as her escort. 'We don't see you often enough in town, and especially in my saloon, the Golden Fleece.'

Miss Millie couldn't resist teasing Charles a little over his non-attendance at her dance hall. Charles was more serious than most of the other young homesteaders who regularly drank and caroused in her bar at weekends. At the same time, Miss Millie felt an affinity for the handsome young man who was accompanying Blanche Fisher. Like him, Millie was not fully accepted by the Anderton establishment. Like him, she flouted convention; though she did so in a flamboyant manner, while Charles maintained a dignified reserve.

Meanwhile, Ian Tanner had joined them. He handed Charles Lynch a glass of red wine.

'You keep your young feller well clear of the Golden Fleece, Blanche,' he said jokingly. 'Miss Millie has turned me down so often, I reckon she must be

waiting for someone like Charles to sweep her up onto his white stallion and ride off with her into the sunset!'

The banker's pleasantries failed to put the young homesteader at ease. He could tell from their glances that most of the guests resented his presence, especially now that Blanche's brother Tess had gone missing. It was common knowledge that Tess disapproved of his sister's friendship with Charles, although the homesteader had never done him any harm.

The gunslinger Mort Lazarus was at the party, shadowing the lady judge, but also finding the time to converse with the prominent businessmen present. Charles Lynch was disappointed that the marshal hadn't showed; although he'd only met Tom Hall briefly he'd taken to the lawman and his down-to-earth manner.

As the guests sat down to dinner, the Rockingstone Hotel began to fill up with friends of Tess Fisher. Word had spread quickly that Carlos was in town,

being wined and dined by their missing friend's own sister.

'My pa's over there with the others,' Duncan Tudball announced. 'I bet he's pig-sick at having to sit at the same table as one of them murdering squatters.'

'We oughta go drag Carlos out of there,' another muttered. 'We oughta teach him a lesson.'

They drank some more before deciding to call in at the Golden Fleece on their way to the banker's house. When they learned that there was no show at the saloon that night because of Miss Millie's absence, their bad temper intensified. By now, Duncan Tudball was their self-appointed leader.

'Let's get out of this stinking whore-house,' he said loudly, smashing his glass on the table as he spoke. 'Let's go and wish that Mexican pig farmer a pleasant evening!'

From his vantage point behind the counter, Joel the giant bartender watched the rabble troop out into the

street. He was almost sorry they hadn't caused more trouble in the saloon; he'd have enjoyed laying a few of them out, even if he'd had to pay for it in the long run.

He didn't like the situation one bit; Miss Millie was at the party and Joel felt responsible for her safety, both in and outside of the Golden Fleece. He wiped his hands on his apron and then hung it up behind the counter. He'd better go and tell the marshal what was going on.

The diners heard the shouting outside in the street; the purpose of the gathering soon became apparent.

'Carlos . . . Carlos. Come out here, you yellow sonofabitch!'

All eyes turned towards the young home-steader, whose face had grown pale and stony. One of the women giggled nervously, adding to the tension everyone felt. Only Mort Lazarus continued eating.

Charles Lynch rose suddenly to his feet. 'Excuse me,' he told Tanner and

Miss Millie. 'I have to be on my way.'

'No, Charles,' Blanche pleaded. 'Stay here with me.'

She tried to grab his arm, but he pulled himself free, and walked out of the silent room.

Ian Tanner followed him into the hallway. 'I'm coming with you, Charles,' he said.

The youngster halted in his tracks. 'No,' he said firmly. 'You'd be doing me a disservice. Thank you for the evening.'

Mort Lazarus could feel Jo Deneuve's gaze on him. He could read her thoughts.

'It's no good,' he told her coldly. 'He shouldn't be here.'

Charles Lynch opened the front door of the house and stepped out onto the verandah. The crowd fell silent for a moment, then Duncan Tudball realized that the homesteader was unarmed.

'We're gonna run you out of town, Carlos,' he yelled. 'We're gonna run you right out of the territory. And we're gonna tar and feather you on the way.'

A great roar went up from the crowd but then a shotgun exploded a few yards behind them. Tom Hall was standing there with a smoking double-barrel in his hands. Next to him stood Joel, holding a further pair of similar weapons at the ready.

'I've got one shot left in this gun,' the lawman warned them. 'And both Joel's guns are loaded with buckshot. Next time I fire, somebody's gonna lose a leg. So git!'

Nobody present thought the marshal was bluffing, least of all Duncan Tudball, who was staring into the nozzles of the shotgun. The crowd disappeared rapidly. When they'd all gone, Tom Hall turned to Charles Lynch.

'I cain't let you go back to your place, Charles,' he said. 'Not for the time being. You'll be safer in the jailhouse where I can watch over you. I'll have a word with Blanche in the morning. She'll make sure you're fed properly.'

16

Next day the inevitable came to pass: a group of volunteers were riding past the entrance to Acorn Creek when the leading rider suggested they turn into the creek and take a look.

'I cain't see Tess venturing off the beaten track like that,' another horseman objected. 'It ain't as if Acorn Creek leads anyplace.'

'If he'd kept to the beaten track he'd have been found by now,' the first man replied with dry logic.

Unwillingly the others followed him into the creek, certain that they were wasting their time.

'Someone's been here,' the leader commented. He'd spotted a hoofprint in the soft earth right at the water's edge.

They came upon the body a hundred yards further on. It was lying on its

stomach where it had been brought down by Mort Lazarus' bullets.

'Jeez,' one of the volunteers muttered. 'It looks like Tess.'

The remains of the rancher's son were not a pretty sight. One side of his face was exposed to the sunlight and had blistered. The carrion crows had been busy too, and the exposed eye socket was a hollow crater. Only the hardiest of the volunteers took a close look.

'He's been shot three times,' one of them said. 'In the back!'

'I don't see no sign of his horse,' someone remarked from the back of the group.

A few of them began to whistle shrilly, but without success.

'I reckon that's why he was killed,' the leading rider said.

The man next to him shook his head. 'Not here,' he said. 'Not in the creek. No horse thief would sit in a God-forsaken spot like this in the hope of someone just happening to come along.

It don't make sense.'

'Well, who d'you reckon, then?'

'Homesteaders. Tess was shot else-where and brought here to cover their tracks.'

The choice of the homesteaders as the killers was a popular one. The assembled men all nodded their heads grimly. None of them had rated Tess Fisher highly during his life, but now he'd become a symbol of their distrust and hatred of the people who lived outside the town — squatters, ren-egades and now murderers.

'We'll have to take him back home,' the leading rider sighed. 'His folk will need to see him before he's buried.'

When they reached Anderton, the cortège halted in front of the Rocking-stone Hotel. Tim Riley was standing on the hotel steps, his face clouded. Tudball, the storekeeper, and other town businessmen were also out on the street, eager to know what was going on.

Tim Riley glanced at the body slung

over the saddle of one of the horses. 'I'll send for Will Fisher,' he said. 'And the lady judge, too.'

A crowd of onlookers gathered in a matter of minutes, men, women and excited children who had to be rebuked sharply to keep quiet.

When the news reached the rancher's house, Mrs Fisher almost collapsed with shock.

'You stay with her, Blanche,' Will Fisher ordered his daughter. 'I've got to go over there.'

Blanche could feel the tears welling up in her eyes, but she knew that she had to be strong. Her father was forcing himself to control his emotions, though his face was ashen.

As he strode along the street, watched by scores of townspeople, the rancher prayed silently that there'd been some mistake, that the corpse they'd brought in was a stranger who merely resembled Tess.

The crowd in front of the Rockingstone Hotel opened up for him and he

caught his first glimpse of the patient horse's burden. His legs went weak and an awful pain gripped his chest. It was Tess all right. He felt Riley and Tudball at his side, supporting him in case he fell.

'I'm sorry, Will,' the saloon keeper told him. 'The whole town's sorry.'

Mort Lazarus had appeared from nowhere and was standing next to the dead youngster. He looked suitably sympathetic as the rancher managed to walk over to his son's body and run his finger through Tess's hair.

For a moment it looked as if the rancher was going to break down and weep, but suddenly he straightened his back and turned to face the group of volunteer riders.

'Thank you,' he said in a hoarse voice. 'Thank you for finding my son.'

At the back of the crowd Jo Deneuve felt a lump in her throat at this awful moment. She was glad that Tom Hall was there at her side like a rock.

Then a man stepped out of the

crowd and addressed Will Fisher. The man was a stranger who'd only turned up in town the day before.

'I saw this young man alive a few days ago,' he said in a Mexican accent that matched his swarthy appearance. 'He was with another man near the entrance to a creek. They were both arguing and quarrelling when I rode by.'

Mort Lazarus took a step forward and faced the stranger.

'Can you describe the other feller?' he asked. 'Did you get a good look at him?'

'Sure I did, *Señor*,' the Mexican replied.

The man's memory for detail was remarkable. By the time he'd finished his description, nobody in the crowd was in any doubt that the mystery rider who'd met and presumably killed Tess Fisher at Acorn Creek was his old enemy, Saul Banks.

17

Marshal Tom Hall was not invited to the emergency meeting of the town council that evening. The gunslinger Lazarus was, but he sat silent for the greater part of the proceedings while the members discussed in heated terms the outrage that had been done to their community.

The hardware merchant, Tudball, chaired the meeting in the absence of rancher Will Fisher who'd decided to stay at home with his distraught family.

'Will Fisher has told me how he feels,' Tudball informed the gathering. 'He wants to see Saul Banks hanged for this. If any homesteader hides or protects the murderer, his property should be burned to the ground.'

The members applauded his strong words. The time for reckoning had arrived.

'We shoulda taken action years ago,' Willis the cobbler said. 'If we had, maybe Tess would be alive today and them cowhands wouldn't have been gunned down on the range.'

Tudball's gaze wandered around the table.

'We ain't all young men,' he pointed out. 'I reckon I'm not too old to join a posse, and I know my son Duncan will come along as well. But some of you are older than me and I don't expect you to spend days in the saddle. I hope you'll play your part, though, by providing horses and ammunition for any volunteers who need them.'

The members nodded their assent, and Tudball's eyes glowed in anticipation of the adventure ahead.

'I reckon we can raise nigh on a score of good men in the town,' he continued. 'And Will Fisher has promised us half a dozen of his cowpokes who can handle a gun.'

At that moment Ian Tanner, the

banker, coughed loudly and rose to his feet.

'Murder is a serious matter,' he told them. 'It should be dealt with in a lawful manner.'

'It'll be lawful all right,' Tim Riley assured him with a short laugh. 'If we bring him in alive the lady judge can sentence him; if he's dead she can arrange a lawful funeral!'

The banker sat down again, stony-faced. Not a single member had supported his call for restraint. Tudball turned to Mort Lazarus who was manicuring his nails with a small file.

'Will Fisher wants you to head the posse, Mort,' he said. 'He's offering you five hundred dollars down payment, to be followed by a further five hundred if the mission succeeds. The men who ride with you will be rewarded as well.'

The gunslinger smiled faintly.

'I accept the offer, Mr Tudball,' he replied. 'Ask Mr Fisher to deposit the money first thing tomorrow morning in Mr Tanner's bank. I'll need a day or

two to reconnoitre the territory alone; you can use that time to enlist men to ride with me when I've laid my plans.'

* * *

While the council meeting was in session, the town marshal was conferring with Jo Deneuve in her office at the other end of the main street.

'I didn't like that Mexican feller's story,' he told her. 'It just don't seem likely that Saul would quarrel openly with Tess Fisher in front of a witness, and later shoot him three times in the back. Saul would know he couldn't get away with it.'

'I agree,' the girl replied. 'Besides, the killing was cowardly, yet Saul took Tess on face to face at the barbecue, and beat him. It was Tess who used underhand methods to even the score.'

The lawman nodded his head thoughtfully. He'd only met Banks briefly, but the youngster had seemed straight and honest.

'I want you to keep out of this, Tom,' the lady judge said suddenly. 'Tempers are running too high for one man to make any difference. I don't want you gunned down by a hothead.'

He felt uncomfortable under her gaze; did she still think he wasn't up to his job?

'I oughta do something,' he objected. 'Even if it's only to call help in from outside.'

'No, Tom,' she said firmly. 'That's up to the town council. You may not even be in a job in a week's time.'

'I guess I cain't stop anyone riding out of town,' the lawman commented. 'But if they do bring a prisoner in, I ain't gonna let them string him up like a dog.'

'And I'll be the first to back you up, Tom,' the girl assured him, though silently she was praying that the situation wouldn't get that bad.

18

The posse finally hit the trail three days later, with the citizens of Anderton lining the main street to wish them God speed.

Will Fisher had buried his son and was hellbent on revenge. He and Tudball the storekeeper rode in the vanguard of the group, together with Mort Lazarus who looked very confident and relaxed.

Word had spread quickly that Saul Banks and a few friends were holed up in Devil's Canyon; if that was true, it might prove costly to winkle them out.

'It's no problem, Mr Fisher,' Lazarus assured the rancher. 'I got it all figured out. We're gonna catch them cold.'

The homesteads they passed were closed and shuttered. None of the settlers were prepared to help them on their way, nor did anyone want to pick a

quarrel with such a large group of men who carried revenge in their hearts.

Dusk found them still a few miles from the canyon. Alby Smith, the ranch foreman, rode alongside the leading riders to offer some advice.

'We'll need to stop soon,' he told them. 'The light's fading and the going's getting rougher. I cain't understand why we didn't leave Anderton before noon.'

Mort Lazarus gave him a cold stare. 'Don't worry about the horses,' he told the foreman. 'They're not going into the canyon tonight. We'll go in on foot and bed down. That way we'll surprise them at first light.'

Alby Smith understood the plan; the canyon twisted and turned for half a mile before opening up into a wooded basin occasionally frequented by sheep and goat herders who'd built crude cabins to protect them against the weather. Saul Banks and his friends were probably holed up in those cabins. If the posse could sneak up on them the

young homesteaders would be caught like rats in a trap.

'You'll need to leave someone to look after the horses,' Smith pointed out.

Tudball looked over his shoulder at his son Duncan. He'd have liked to keep the youngster out of danger, but Duncan forestalled him.

'I ain't staying with no horses,' he said. 'I'm going along with you, Pa.'

'You can stay with the horses, Smith,' Mort Lazarus told the foreman.

Alby Smith glanced across at Will Fisher. The rancher merely nodded his head to confirm what he'd already said: the gunslinger Mort Lazarus was in charge until they'd hunted Saul Banks down.

Will Fisher had a troubled night's sleep wrapped in his blanket under the stars. The face of his dead son kept reappearing in his dreams, and each time he awoke he felt the familiar ache in his heart.

He felt someone shaking his shoulders gently. It was Tudball who'd woken

with the crack of dawn.

'Lazarus has gone,' the storekeeper informed him tersely. 'My boy's been looking for him, but he ain't here.'

Will Fisher shivered as he threw the blanket to one side.

'Don't panic,' he said with a yawn. 'He's probably gone scouting.'

Above them, concealed on the craggy slopes of the gorge, Saul Banks and his companions were well placed to observe every move the intruders made. Saul had never really believed that Mort Lazarus would fulfill his promise to deliver the posse into his hands, but now the unbelievable had happened. Yet despite Mort's obvious goodwill Saul still couldn't figure the gunslinger out.

'I just want to see justice done,' Mort Lazarus had told him a few days earlier. 'You're being blamed for a killing I don't reckon you did. When you've got Will Fisher and his men in your rifle sights, maybe they'll parley and listen to reason.'

Saul watched the remainder of the vigilantes stir from their blankets and sleeping-bags and stretch their stiff limbs in the pale morning light. Now was as good a time as any to start proceedings. He moved out from behind a large boulder, his rifle laid flat across his arm.

'Fisher,' he yelled. 'Will Fisher. You and me need to talk.'

His words echoed around the canyon and the posse froze as they scanned the slopes above them.

'Don't do anything foolish,' Saul warned them. 'You're covered by half a dozen rifles.'

His companion moved into view to reinforce the point he was making.

Young Duncan Tudball felt his blood run cold as he caught sight of the sharpshooters; they definitely were no figment of Saul Banks' imagination.

Will Fisher shielded his eyes as he stared up at Banks.

'You killed my son,' he accused him in a voice that trembled with anger.

135

'You shot him down from behind like a dog.'

Before Saul could answer the accusation a shot rang out and one of Will Fisher's cowpokes crumpled to the ground. Startled, Saul turned his head to see which of his friends had been crazy enough to open fire without cause. Then a bullet ricocheted against the boulder near his head and made him dive for cover.

In the heat of the moment the majority of the vigilantes forgot how vulnerable they were and began firing wildly into the rocks above their heads. They soon began to pay the price for their lack of caution. Another of Fisher's cowhands fell with a bullet in the neck and a townsman who tried to tend to him had his spine shattered a few moments later.

Duncan Tudball was so frightened that he didn't even draw his gun. He'd anticipated a rabbit-shoot, but not with himself as the rabbit. The homesteaders were expert rifle shots.

'Dad, Dad, where are you?' he yelled in the confusion of gunshots, screaming and cursing. He collided with an older man who was trying to take aim with his revolver. The man shoved the youngster to one side but was cut down before he could relocate his target.

'Dad, Dad . . . ' Duncan stumbled drunkenly among the wounded and dying. He passed Will Fisher, who still stood erect, pumping lead into the canyon wall.

From the comparative safety of a huge rock, Tudball the storekeeper watched his son's erratic course and screamed at the boy to take cover. The din of the firing ceased for a brief instant and Duncan seemed to pick out his father's voice.

'Over here,' Tudball yelled. 'Over here, Goddam you!'

Duncan turned in the direction of the rock and saw his father's upraised arm. The youngster smiled with relief and then a rifle shot shattered his rib-cage just below the heart.

'Duncan, Duncan . . . '

The storekeeper forgot his own safety and rushed out into the open. Duncan was lying on his back on the brown earth, blood trickling from his mouth. In the meantime Will Fisher's Colt had jammed. Seeing Tudball crouched down by his son's body, Fisher went up to him and demanded his gun.

Tudball was too shocked to respond and Fisher shook him vigorously by the shoulder. Then a fierce salvo of shots rang out and both men keeled over.

Tudball had caught a slug in the lung and he knew with a sense of relief that he was following Duncan into the afterlife. With his remaining strength he reached out and held his son's hand for the last time. Then there was silence.

19

When ranch foreman Alby Smith brought news of the disaster to Anderton, the first man he turned to for help was Marshal Tom Hall.

'God knows who started the shooting,' Smith said. 'I was at the mouth of the canyon with the horses. When I got to them, the two Tudballs were dead and about a dozen others. Will Fisher and a few more are badly hurt. I had to leave them there, but I did manage to bring one feller back who was able to mount his horse. I've left him at the doc's place. I called at the ranch-house on the way and I've sent a couple of cowhands along to tend to the wounded and get them to a safe place.'

'What about Lazarus?' Tom Hall asked.

'I didn't see him there,' Smith replied. 'Only the homesteaders who'd

done the shooting. They rode past me and out of the canyon. I thought they might gun me down, but they left me in peace. They just wanted to get out of there as fast as they could.'

Outside in the street a crowd had gathered.

'I guess I'd better let them know what's happened,' Smith said. 'I'd better call on Mrs Fisher, too.'

Despite his concern for the townsfolk Tom Hall was thinking about Charles Lynch who was still in the jailhouse. Anderton was no safe place for a homesteader at a time like this.

'Tell the men to take some buckboards out to Devil's Canyon,' he told Smith. 'I'm gonna take Lynch out the back way. I'll go straight to the canyon and see what I can do until the townsfolk get there.'

Hall was lucky enough to get Charles Lynch away from the jail without being seen by a hostile eye. But the young homesteader was uneasy as they rode out of town.

'I should call and see Blanche,' he muttered. 'She'll be worried sick about her pa.'

'She'll be even more worried if some fool tries to take a shot at you,' the lawman pointed out. 'I want to see you safely back on your own patch. I'll let you know when it's OK for you to visit Blanche in Anderton.'

They parted company two miles outside of town. The young homesteader watched the marshal ride away into the distance and wished he was going with him; but he knew that it was crazy even to think about it.

His attention was soon distracted from his gloomy thoughts by a group of riders coming along the trail towards him. When they got closer he recognized Mort Lazarus and a half-dozen companions who looked as if they'd been living rough for weeks. Two or three of them were Mexicans, or at least swarthy enough to be so.

Mort Lazarus settled his gaze on the young homesteader for the briefest of

moments and then let it stray away contemptuously. Lynch wondered what he was doing with these strangers when he was meant to be at Devil's Canyon with the posse of townsfolk.

However, one of the Mexicans took a greater interest in the youngster and turned his horse towards him.

'Carlos,' he exclaimed. 'Carlos Lynch!'

Charles stared at him blankly and the man grinned through his heavy beard.

'You don't know me because I have not shaved for weeks, Carlos,' he said. 'But I have stayed at your house in El Paso. My name is Santos. I'm an old friend of your father. Do you remember me now?'

Charles nodded his head. A lot of his father's old friends had stayed at their home, many of them carrying slugs from skirmishes with the law. He recalled that Santos had been more civil than most of them, and had shown his mother some courtesy and gratitude for her hospitality.

Santos turned to Mort Lazarus.

'This muchacho's father was a fast gun, Mort,' he said. 'Almost as fast as you.'

'That was before he started drinking,' Charles commented bitterly.

'What about you, Carlos?' the Mexican enquired. 'if you're like your father I could use you along with us.'

'I'm not like my father,' Charles said quietly. 'I'm a farmer and that's what I intend to stay.'

Mort Lazarus had reached the end of his patience.

'Let's get going, Santos,' he said. 'I'm looking forward to a hot bath.'

20

Events moved quickly over the next couple of days. As the town mourned its dead and tended the wounds of the survivors of the ill-fated posse, Lazarus and the rest of the outlaws installed themselves in the Rockingstone Hotel as the uninvited and unwelcome guests of saloon owner Tim Riley.

The mood of the township was dominated by the shock of the massacre at Devil's Canyon and the foreboding aroused by the presence of Santos' gang. Everybody realized that the newcomers had no honest or honourable motives for being in Anderton at this particular time.

Santos himself could hardly conceal his satisfaction at the way things had turned out.

'You are a brilliant man, Mort,' he congratulated the gunslinger over a

bottle of whiskey in Lazarus' hotel room. 'We killed three cowhands out on the range and Anderton's best men were gunned down thanks to our intervention at the canyon. Yet nobody can prove anything against us. In the meantime Saul Banks and his friends have fled the territory for fear of the law. This town is ours to do what we like with.'

'We were lucky,' Lazarus pointed out. 'Things would have been a lot trickier if that girl hadn't got herself killed in the first place.'

'Trickier, yes,' the Mexican agreed, 'but not impossible. We'd have made our own luck, Mort.'

Lazarus wandered over to the window and looked out onto the main street. The jailhouse caught his eye and made him frown.

'I'm going downstairs to have a word with Riley,' he informed Santos. 'It's about time the town council held a meeting . . . '

The meeting was convened for the

145

following afternoon in the small, single-storey building that served as the town hall. It was poorly attended since several of the members had not returned in one piece from Devil's Canyon. Mort Lazarus and Santos presented themselves as delegates on behalf of the wounded rancher Will Fisher who was being nursed by his wife and daughter at their town house.

From the chair, Tim Riley welcomed the two delegates. Nobody was pleased to see them there, but it had not escaped members' notice that Santos had posted two of his men at the entrance to the hall to remind them of the transfer of power in the township.

Chairman Tim Riley opened the meeting and called on Mort Lazarus to report on the disaster at Devil's Canyon. Lazarus was well prepared for this moment, since it was he who'd drawn up the agenda and presented it to Riley as a *fait accompli*.

'I'd ridden off for help from Santos here,' the gunslinger informed the

gathering without batting an eyelid. 'The posse decided to fight it out with the homesteaders before we could get back to them.'

Alone of all the members present, banker Ian Tanner spoke his doubts aloud. 'Didn't you tell Will Fisher to wait for your return?' he asked.

'I told him I had a plan,' Lazarus replied coldly. 'He didn't ask me to fill in the details.'

Nobody else spoke up so the matter was dropped in favour of the next item on the agenda: the election of a new town marshal.

Tim Riley's face was rather pale as he remembered the conversation he'd already had on the subject with Mort Lazarus. He avoided eye contact with the other members as he informed them that the gunslinger had been proposed for marshal.

'Well, I propose our present lawman, Tom Hall,' Ian Tanner said without hesitation. 'He's done a splendid job for us this far.'

If he was hoping for backing he was sorely disappointed. His words were greeted with a gloomy silence. Then the Mexican Santos drew his Colt from his holster and laid it flat on the table in front of him.

'I suggest that you take a vote on it, *Señores*,' he said. 'Then you can all get back to your families.'

21

Tom Hall was determined not to spend his last few hours as lawman skulking in his office at the jailhouse. Instead, he visited the homes of each of the injured possemen in turn to make sure that their families were not in need of anything.

His last port of call was Will Fisher's house, a large, detached villa on the outskirts of town. Blanche Fisher opened the front door to him and explained that the maid was taking her turn of duty at the rancher's bedside, while Mrs Fisher was upstairs resting.

'How's your father doing?' Hall enquired.

'He's getting stronger,' the girl assured him, 'but the doctor says it will take weeks before he's on his feet again.'

The marshal stood there awkwardly

until Blanche thought to ask him inside.

'No, it's OK, thanks,' Hall said. 'I just wanted to know how your pa was. I gotta be getting back to the jailhouse.'

The girl hesitated. 'How's Charles?' she asked. 'I haven't seen him in days.'

'I guess that's my fault, Miss Fisher,' the lawman apologized. 'I've told him to steer clear of Anderton for the time being.'

'You did right, Marshal, and I'm grateful to you for everything,' she told him. 'But if you do see Charles, tell him . . . '

Her voice trailed off. Her whole life seemed to be going to pieces. Her brother dead, her father wounded, and Charles in danger maybe.

'I'll tell him,' Tom Hall said gently. 'I know he's thinking about you, too, Miss Fisher.'

He retraced his steps to the jail along a very quiet main street. Anderton's usual vitality had been sapped by recent events. It was like a ghost town.

He turned a corner and almost collided with a member of the town council. The meeting must have ended. Tom Hall could guess the result of the vote by the shifty way the man diverted his gaze and went on his way with a mumbled salutation.

'So that's that,' the lawman thought bitterly. 'I just hope they pay me what I'm owed!'

He felt a pang of regret as he went inside the jailhouse. It had only been his home for a few weeks, but they'd been the most eventful weeks of his whole life. He gathered his belongings together and sat down to wait for someone to inform him officially of his dismissal.

To his surprise the news was broken to him not by Tim Riley or Ian Tanner, but by Jo Deneuve the lady judge.

'It's not good news, Tom,' she told him, placing a sheet of paper on the table in front of him. He didn't even bother to read it.

'It's not news at all, Jo,' he

commented with a wry smile. 'I been expecting to get voted out.'

'Only Ian Tanner supported you,' Jo said. 'But he did manage to get them to pay you an extra week's salary for all you've done for the town.'

'I guess I didn't do enough to hold my job,' Tom said.

'Not after Santos put his gun on the desk and invited members to vote,' Jo replied. 'Mort Lazarus takes over as marshal from midnight.'

'Lazarus,' Tom mused aloud. 'Well, at least it's someone you can work with, Jo.'

The girl's eyes flashed angrily and he regretted his remark immediately. It was stupid and unfair of him to vent his bitterness on Jo Deneuve.

'I shan't be working with Mort Lazarus,' she informed him coldly. 'I've already handed in my resignation to the town council in protest at the way you've been treated. I shall continue to work for the citizens of Anderton in a private capacity. Anticipating a fall in

income I'm leaving my room in the Rockingstone Hotel. Miss Millie has offered me accommodation at her place at a cheaper rate.'

Tom could think of nothing to say except to ask her why she'd been chosen to break the news to him of his dismissal.

'It was Ian Tanner's idea,' she said. 'He's hoping you'll listen to me.'

'Listen to you . . . about what?'

'You've got to get out of town, Tom. You've got to get out now!'

He stared at her. 'Why should I leave?' he asked.

She moved closer to him and he could smell the fragrance of her perfume.

'The town council's caved in to Mort's demands,' she said. 'Ian says you're the only man the townsfolk could rally to. Santos and the other outlaws know that, Tom. If you don't leave, they'll kill you.'

Suddenly she was in his arms and he was holding her tight.

'I won't run,' he whispered. 'I've never run.'

She tilted her head and let him kiss her on the lips. Then she pulled away from him.

'Well do it for me, Tom,' she begged him. 'Do it because I love you . . .'

★　★　★

Ian Tanner was still in Jo Deneuve's office when she got back.

'How did he take it?' he asked.

The girl shrugged her shoulders. She looked tired and sad.

'He took it,' she said. 'But I don't think he'll go too far away. I guess he feels he's part of the town by now, despite what they've done to him.'

The banker took a large cigar out of his breast pocket, lit it and savoured the flavour.

'Anderton only means something to Tom because you happen to be here, Jo,' he told her.

She gave a wry smile at that.

'It's not really the best of times to form attachments, is it?' she observed.

'Nope, it isn't,' Tanner agreed. He picked up a piece of paper from the desk. 'That's why I've been writing down a few observations while you were over at the jailhouse. A kind of last will and testament, if you like.'

The girl sat down behind the desk and waited for him to explain himself.

'I've no illusions as to why Lazarus and Santos are in Anderton,' Tanner said. 'I know what kind of men they are. They are here to plunder the township and our illustrious citizens have played into their hands. The main objective of such bandits is money and the bank is the obvious target.'

Jo Deneuve listened to him in silence. So far all her concerns had centred on Tom Hall.

'I want to draw up a document leaving all my possessions to Miss Millie,' Tanner said. 'You see, I am determined to defend my bank even at the cost of my life.'

He studied the cigar for a moment, watching the blue smoke curl upwards.

'I also want to put the record straight for Miss Millie,' he said. 'She has always considered me something of a gentleman — and a rather staid gentleman at that. In fact, I worked for years as a professional gambler in the seedier establishments of San Francisco. My two cashiers at the bank also earned their living at the gaming tables before we all decided to present ourselves here as honest businessmen and launch a bank in a growing township.'

His eyes had a hard glint in them now, and his chin jutted out defiantly.

'In short, Jo,' he told the girl. 'If me and my staff are going to get killed in the line of duty, you can be sure that we shall take more than one of Mort Lazarus' gang to hell with us . . . '

22

Mort Lazarus would have liked a few weeks to settle in as town marshal and suss out the best way to exploit the situation. But he soon saw that things were not going to go according to plan. The main problem was Santos; Lazarus had known the Mexican off and on for nearly ten years and they'd occasionally teamed up and committed robberies and even killings.

Santos had always been reliable and cautious, a cool head in any predicament. When they'd met up in Tucson a few months earlier to discuss the Anderton venture the Mexican had seemed as sharp as always, yet the band of men he'd chosen to bring with him were a wild, motley bunch and they seemed to have communicated some of their less desirable qualities to Santos during the time they'd spent out on the

range fomenting trouble between the homesteaders and Will Fisher's cowhands.

The other two Mexicans, Valdes and Guillen, were sensible enough but Larkins from Ohio and Peach and Fielding from Texas had done nothing but drink and gamble since they arrived at the Rockingstone Hotel, and unfortunately Santos had fallen in with the Americans' reckless lifestyle rather than stick by his more sober compatriots.

Tim Riley's hotel lost its popularity when the outlaw gang moved in; in fact it became more like a morgue than a saloon. To relieve the monotony Santos and the three Americans played interminable card games and consumed bottle after bottle of Tim Riley's rye whiskey in the process.

Matters came to a head on the morning of their sixth day in town. Hungover from the previous night, Peach lost heavily to Santos and Larkins. Long before noon he was in debt to the tune of several hundred

dollars — money he didn't possess.

'And don't forget the twenty-four dollars you owe me from last night,' Larkins reminded the Texan.

Peach gazed at him with jaundiced eyes.

'The hell with you, Larkins,' he snapped. 'I been sleeping rough for weeks and I ain't got two dimes to show for it.'

Mort Lazarus stood quietly at the bar watching the gamblers. He knew better than to interfere in an argument between drunks.

'Calm down, Peach,' Santos warned the Texan. 'If you don't like losing don't play in the first place.'

Peach picked up the cards and threw them across the table.

'I play 'cos I'm bored,' he grumbled. 'If I had some real money I could get myself a good time far away from this hell-hole.'

Fielding took a swig of whiskey and belched raucously.

'I know where there's real money,' he

said. 'Over at the bank.'

The four players looked thoughtful for a moment. Mort Lazarus chose that moment to issue some advice.

'Put that idea out of your heads,' he told them.

Fielding's eyes narrowed. The Texan resented being ordered about, and especially by a phoney town marshal.

'Relax, Mort,' Santos said with a sly smile. 'All that Fielding is saying is that a bank is a good place to ask for a loan.'

The remark went down well with his fellow gamblers.

'You're right, you goddam Mex,' Larkins congratulated him. 'Let's go down to the bank and talk to one of them old walruses who run the place. Ain't no harm in that, is there?'

The men rose to their feet and started for the door. Lazarus knew that he'd lost the initiative. To stop them now he'd have to draw his gun and that would be suicidal.

Santos turned to the two Mexicans, who were playing dice near the window.

Guillen was his closest friend and he got up obediently, whereas Valdes remained in his seat.

'What about you, Valdes?' Larkins asked challengingly.

The Mexican had already made up his mind. He didn't much like Mort Lazarus but he knew that the gun-slinger was thinking straighter than the rest of them.

'I stay,' Valdes replied quietly. 'I don't need no loan.'

Blanche Fisher was doing the morning shopping when she saw the group of men walking unsteadily past her in the direction of the bank. She sought a shady spot on the sidewalk so that they wouldn't notice her.

Suddenly she felt a presence at her side. It was Mort Lazarus, the man who'd led her father and the townsmen into the trap at Devil's Canyon.

'I'd be honoured if you'd join me for an aperitif at the Rockingstone Hotel, Miss Fisher,' the gunslinger said with an inscrutable smile.

She felt a shiver run through her body.

'Thank you, Mr Lazarus,' she replied. 'But I'd rather not.'

His hand reached out and seized her arm like a vice.

'I'm afraid I must insist, Blanche,' he told her. 'We have many things to discuss.'

★　★　★

Ian Tanner heard the double tap on the door and swivelled his head as Glanville, the senior cashier, sidled into his office.

'I think this is it,' Glanville informed him tersely. 'They're heading this way.'

Tanner nodded his head and Glanville returned to his place behind the counter. Roberts, the other cashier, was already locking the drawers that held the day's cash.

Peach and Larkins were the first into the bank, followed closely by Santos and Fielding. Guillen wisely lingered on

the threshold, awaiting developments. Fortified by Tim Riley's whiskey, Peach walked over to the counter and addressed Glanville insolently.

'Hey you, walrus face,' he snarled. 'I need a loan of five hundred greenbacks. Now!'

The cashier explained in an apologetic tone of voice that the bank needed collateral before it could make a loan. It took a moment for the message to sink into the outlaws' fuddled brains.

'Now that ain't friendly of you, mister,' Larkins chipped in. 'You aiming to make my friend here look like a welcher? What do you reckon, Peach — are you a welcher or what? Are you gonna get us that money you owe us?'

Goaded by Larkins' remarks Peach decided to back up his demands with hardware. But before his Colt cleared the holster the second cashier levelled a .44 at him and shot him straight through the stomach.

Fielding reacted immediately, drawing smoothly and thumbing a shot that

shattered Roberts' elbow before the cashier could fire a second time.

Meanwhile Glanville had retreated behind a heavy cabinet and all the bandits could do was pump lead into the woodwork and keep him pinned down. Roberts had vanished from sight, too; he was crouched on the floor as close as he could squeeze to the counter, his right arm oozing blood.

As Santos and Larkins fired wildly, Fielding spotted the door marked MANAGER. It looked full of possibilities and he advanced on it, keeping a wary eye out for movement on the other side of the counter. Before he reached the door it swung open and he was confronted by Ian Tanner holding a double-barrel shotgun. The banker emptied a barrel into the intruder and Fielding was blown clean off his feet. Tanner fired again and Santos screamed with pain as the pellets tore the flesh from his thigh.

The manager's door slammed shut

again as Tanner paused to reload. Thinking he was caught between two firing-points Larkins turned to face the new danger, thus exposing his back to the original enemy, Glanville. With little concern for chivalry the cashier came out from behind the cabinet and emptied his Colt into the robber's spine.

Santos felt Guillen's left arm encircle his waist.

'Vamos, Guillen,' he muttered through his pain. 'Vamos!'

Even as he spoke Guillen fired into the bank and Glanville slumped against the counter.

'Now we can go,' Guillen said coolly, though the sweat was flowing down his face.

The two Mexicans retreated as best they could down the street towards the safety of the Rockingstone Hotel. Ian Tanner did not pursue them. He had achieved his objective of saving the bank; now he had his two cashiers to think about. Both were hurt.

For a few minutes the two outlaws were at the mercy of anyone in the township who wanted to make a name for himself. As it was, nobody dared. Nobody had the guts.

23

Charles Lynch was carrying a bucket of river water across the yard when he heard the approaching rider. He shielded his eyes against the early afternoon sun and saw that it was the big man who'd helped save him from the mob in Anderton.

Joel was almost as breathless as the powerful gelding he was riding.

'Carlos,' he said. 'You gotta come with me.'

'Why?' the young homesteader demanded. 'What's wrong?'

'There's been shooting in town,' Joel informed him and Lynch's blood ran cold as he thought of Blanche.

'Was anybody hurt?' he asked anxiously.

'Two of Mr Tanner's cashiers were hit,' Joel said. 'Santos and his men tried to take the bank. Three of them were

killed and Santos got it in the leg.'

Charles Lynch wondered why anyone would ride out of town to tell him about a shoot-out at the bank. He began to feel more and more uneasy.

'It was Mr Tanner who sent me,' the big man explained. 'Santos has been telling folks that he used to ride with your father. Tanner wants you to try to talk to Santos and Lazarus and try to persuade them to leave Anderton peaceably.'

Suddenly Tom Hall emerged through the doorway of the cabin, carrying a rifle in his hand. Joel was surprised to see him.

'Marshal!' he said. 'What are you doing here?'

Tom Hall ignored the question, and asked one of his own.

'What's going on in town, Joel?' What help does Tanner need?'

The big man swallowed hard; he knew he'd have to break the news sooner or later.

'They're holding Blanche Fisher in the Rockingstone Hotel,' he said. 'They reckon they're gonna kill her if they don't get the key to the bank and safe passage out of town . . . '

* * *

It was a strange council of war that met later that afternoon at the Fisher residence on the edge of town. Will Fisher himself was propped up in his bed, white-faced and gaunt. With him in the room was Tim Riley, who'd been ejected from his own hotel by the gunslinger Lazarus. Also there was Ian Tanner who'd made arrangements for the doctor to tend the wounds of Glanville and Roberts, whose lives were fortunately not in danger.

The latest arrivals were Tom Hall, Charles Lynch and Joel the bartender, who'd come galloping in from the homestead. In another room Miss Millie and Jo Deneuve were trying to soothe the anxieties of Blanche's

mother, whose nerves were at breaking-point.

'I sent word out to the ranch,' Tim Riley explained to the others. 'Unfortunately, Alby and the rest of the cowhands are working the range, so there's no way they can get here today.'

'What's the situation at the Rocking-stone?' Tom Hall enquired.

'I saw them take Blanche upstairs and lock her in one of the rooms,' Tim Riley replied. 'The room's got a balcony but there's no way down. If she tried to jump, she'd kill herself.'

'Can we get up to the balcony?' Tom Hall asked him.

'No way. The room's immediately above the saloon. You'd need a ladder and they'd gun you down through the saloon window.'

'You say you want me to speak to Santos,' Charles said. 'Where will that get us? Him and Lazarus are killers.'

'In the last resort we'll give them the money,' Ian Tanner replied. 'But Santos will have to convince you that Blanche

won't be harmed.'

Then Will Fisher spoke, but faintly and hoarsely so that they had to strain to hear him.

'I'll pay anything to save my child,' he said and paused momentarily for breath. 'I thank you all. I've been a damn fool. Forgive me.'

Meanwhile, Tom Hall was turning the problem over in his mind.

'Is there a blank wall at your hotel, Riley?' he asked.

'Sure, the west wall; there's just an alleyway outside.'

'Then that's the way we'll go,' Hall informed them. 'Just Joel and me. We'll use a ladder to get onto the roof. Joel can lower me by rope down to the balcony. From then on it's up to me.'

'What about me?' Charles Lynch enquired.

'You and I will go and talk to Santos and Lazarus,' Ian Tanner said. 'Tim Riley can stay here and look after the womenfolk. That way we'll cover as many eventualities as we can.'

When Ian Tanner and Charles Lynch walked into the saloon of the Rocking-stone Hotel only Santos and Mort Lazarus were there to greet them. Ian Tanner wished he could warn Tom Hall that there were two men upstairs guarding Blanche Fisher. Santos was seated at one of the tables, his leg roughly bandaged and stretched out in front of him. Lazarus was standing at the counter, cradling a glass of beer in his left hand. The gunslinger looked confident and relaxed like a gambler with a fistful of aces.

'Carlos,' the Mexican greeted him with false affability. 'So you've come to see how I am, and you've brought your friend to apologize for what he did to my leg.'

'I've come to take Blanche Fisher to safety,' Charles replied in an even tone. 'She's my woman, Santos.'

Santos spread his hands wide in a gesture of helplessness.

'That will be difficult, amigo,' he warned the youngster. 'If you make a false move, Lazarus will kill you. Besides, there are two of my men outside Señorita Fisher's room. At the least sign of trouble they have orders to carry out our original threat . . . '

The ascent of the roof had been easy, but Tom Hall held his breath as Joel used his considerable strength to lower him slowly so that his feet would land gently on the boards of the balcony below. Hall was uncomfortably aware that if Blanche's captors were in the room with her his chances of survival were less than slim.

His feet touched the woodwork and he released his hold on the rope. He peered through the net curtain adorning the french windows and could make out the shape of a girl sitting on the bed. Satisfied that she was alone in the room he tapped gently on the glass until he attracted her attention. She rose to her feet and came over to the window.

With rising tension Tom Hall watched her as she tried to open the door from the inside. It was jammed or locked and didn't yield to her. Then she turned round as if something had startled her. The inner door of the bedroom, the one leading to the corridor, had opened wide to expose the silhouette of a man. Tom Hall drew his gun and kicked hard against the join of the french windows . . .

★ ★ ★

Everyone in the saloon bar stiffened as the shot rang out on the upper floor. Mort Lazarus turned to face Charles Lynch.

'Your woman is dead, Carlos,' he said contemptuously. 'Go back to your farm.'

He half-turned away as if he'd lost all interest in the proceedings. Santos was watching the gunslinger with fascination. Mort's every word and gesture were luring the inexperienced youngster into

a fight he couldn't win. In different circumstances Santos might have warned his old compadre's son against the danger, but now he knew that his own survival depended on Carlos Lynch's death.

Lynch was watching Mort's every movement too, but he wasn't seeing a gunslinger, not even a man because Lazarus was too low to be called a man. The coldness of the homesteader's fury had reduced his opponent to the status of a target, worth no more than one of the tin cans he perched on the wall behind his cabin.

He saw the faint smile on the gunslinger's lips, the dreamy look in his eyes, and the sudden blur as Mort's Colt left the holster. It was such a close call. Glass shattered behind Lynch's head as Mort's shot went wide. Then Mort Lazarus was pirouetting like a puppet, desperately trying to steady himself by reaching out for the smooth mahogany of the counter.

The gunslinger still hadn't let go of

his Colt, so Lynch fired again and this time Lazarus fell heavily on the ground, blood pumping from his mouth.

Another shot rang out and a bottle flew off the table a few feet from where Ian Tanner was standing. He glanced up and saw Guillen crouched at the top of the staircase. Tanner drew and fired, almost simultaneously with Charles Lynch. Both of them saw chunks of wood fly from the rail at the outlaw's side. He's a cool customer, Tanner thought with grudging admiration, as Guillen held his ground. Then Lynch aimed again and for a split second the banker saw a hole open up where Guillen's nose had been and the Mexican fell back onto the thick carpet, his legs twitching as they dangled down over the stairs.

They turned their attention back towards Santos, who seemed to be trying to rearrange the bandage on his thigh, complaining all the time about the pain. Charles Lynch turned to say

something to Tanner but before he could speak the banker had pushed him violently to one side.

The derringer Santos had drawn from the bandage cracked once and Ian Tanner felt a sharp, burning sensation on the outer arm. The bullet had been intended for the young homesteader's heart, but the former gambler had been alert to it.

Santos found himself staring into the barrel of Lynch's .45 and his whole body froze. Lynch had thumbed the hammer but hesitated to release it and kill his father's friend. Ian Tanner had no such compunction and, anyway, his shoulder was hurting him. He shot the Mexican clean through the chest at close range, killing him instantly, which was all the compassion he intended to show the outlaw.

Throwing caution to the wind, Charles Lynch raced up the stairs past the inert form of Guillen. He kicked open the first door he came to and came to a halt as he saw the gun

pointed at his stomach.

Fortunately, the gun in question belonged to Tom Hall who was determined to defend the kidnapped girl to the bitter end. Lynch had to step over the lifeless body of Valdes to reach Blanche, to take her in his arms and to hear her tell him between sobs of happiness that she loved him.

★ ★ ★

The next morning Tom Hall visited the banker at his home and found him in good spirits and well on the way to recovery from the bullet wound in his upper arm. The only complaint Tanner had was that he'd been unable to open the bank for business as usual.

'Well, I guess it's better to have a closed bank than a robbed bank,' Tom Hall remarked philosophically.

'It's just that I cain't arrange a loan for you till I'm back at work,' Tanner said.

Tom Hall stared at him in surprise.

'Loan?' he said. 'I ain't asked for no loan.'

'Nope, you haven't,' the banker agreed. 'Jo Deneuve did that for you. We all know you've dreamed about owning a hardware store of your own one day, Tom. Well, this is your chance. Jo was thinking in terms of a low interest loan; in face she was thinking about a loan with no interest at all, and I'm happy to go along with that after all you've done for this town. Stick around, Tom. Anderton needs you, and so does Jo Deneuve.'

Tom Hall coughed with embarrassment and changed the subject.

'Charles Lynch has agreed to fill in as town marshal for a while,' he said. 'He's gonna try to patch things up between the townsfolk and the homesteaders.'

Tanner nodded his approval. Social harmony was good for business.

'They'll all get a chance to mix at the wedding,' the banker said. 'Nobody'll get excluded; there'll be invitations for everyone.'

'Wedding?' Tom commented. 'What, Charles and Blanche? I thought they'd have waited till Will Fisher got better before announcing something like that.'

'Not Charles and Blanche,' Tanner corrected him. 'Nor you and Jo even. I'm talking about me and Miss Millie. Now that Millie knows that I wasn't a staid old banker all my life but a hardliving gambler, she just cain't wait to hogtie me and make an honest feller of me!'

THE END

A TOWN CALLED TROUBLESOME

John Dyson

Matt Matthews had carved his ranch out of the wild Wyoming frontier. But he had his troubles. The big blow of '86 was catastrophic, with dead beeves littering the plains, and the oncoming winter presaged worse. On top of this, a gang of desperadoes had moved into the Snake River valley, killing, raping and rustling. All Matt can do is to take on the killers single-handed. But will he escape the hail of lead?

SMOKING STAR

B. J. Holmes

In the one-horse town of Medicine Bluff two men were dead. Sheriff Jack Starr didn't need the badge on his chest to spur him into tracking the killer. He had his own reason for seeking justice, a reason no-one knew. It drove him to take a journey into the past where he was to discover something else that was to add even greater urgency to the situation — to stop Montana's rivers running red with blood.

CABEL

Paul K. McAfee

Josh Cabel returned home from the Civil War to find his family all murdered by rioting members of Quantrill's band. The hunt for the killers led Josh to Colorado City where, after months of searching, he finally settled down to work on a ranch nearby. He saved the life of an Indian, who led him to a cache of weapons waiting for Sitting Bull's attack on the Whites. His involvement threw Cabel into grave danger. When the final confrontation came, who had the fastest — and deadlier — draw?